YOUTH

GOVERNOR GENERAL'S LITERARY AWARDS
ENGLISH: CHILDREN'S TEXT.

1975   Freeman, Bill.

Shantymen of Cache Lake.

Shantymen of Cache Lake

Shantymen of Cache Lake

Bill Freeman

James Lorimer & Company, Publishers
Toronto   1975

ISBN 0-88862-090-x paper
    0-88862-091-8 cloth

Cover illustration: John Boyle
Design: Lynn Campbell

Photo credits
Public Archives of Canada: 1, 7, 9,11,13,14, 15, 17,18,19.
Notman Photographic Archives, McCord Museum, McGill
  University: 3, 10, 12, 20.
 Ontario Archives: 8.
Charles Macnamara Collection, Ontario Archives: 2, 4, 5, 6. Mr.
Muirhead and the Arnprior and District Museum: 16

James Lorimer & Company, Publishers
Egerton Ryerson Memorial Building
35 Britain Street
Toronto
11 10   86

Canadian Cataloguing in Publication Data
Freeman, Bill
  Shantymen of Cache Lake.

ISBN0-88862-091-8. ISBNO-88862-090-X pbk.

1. Lumbering - Ontario - Juvenile fiction. 2. Lumber camps - Ontario - Juvenile fiction. 1. Title.
PS8561.R388S5   813'.54
PR9199.3.F

This is a story of the adventures of two young people working in a lumber camp in the Ottawa Valley in the 1870s. The characters in this book are all fictional, but everything else is real. The towns, roads, rivers, the shanties, the work of the shantymen, and their attempts to protect themselves by organizing a union—all this is a matter of historical fact.

The photographs portray the square timber trade in Canada in the 1870s. Here you can see the shanties, the cambooses, the squared timber, the rafts, and finally the ships which took the timber to England. In this book I have tried to make this setting come alive, so that readers can experience in their imagination what it was really like for the thousands of Canadians who worked "in the shanties" a hundred years ago.

B. F.

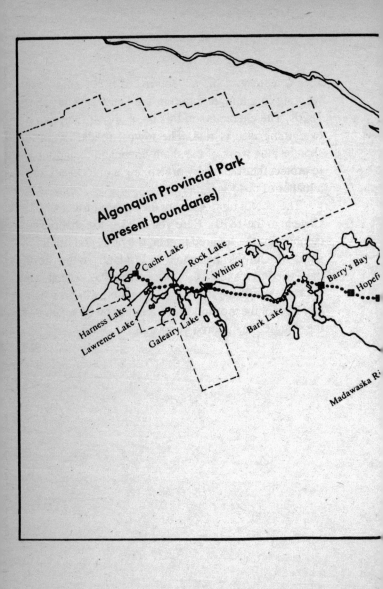

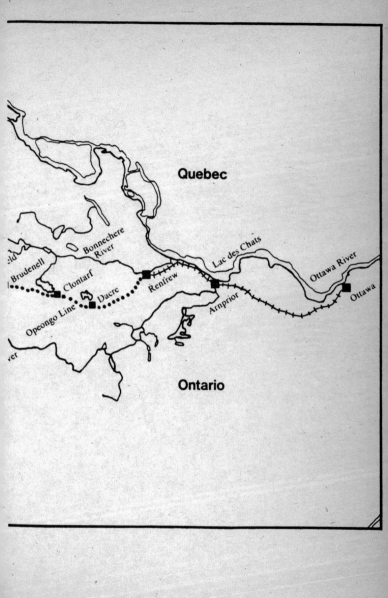

The Lumber Camp Song

Come all you jolly fellows and listen to my song;
It's all about the shanty boys and how they get along,
We're the joiliest bunch of fellows that ever you could find;
The way we spend our winter months is hurling down the pine.

At four o'clock each morning the boss begins to shout:
"Heave out my jolly teamsters; it's time to start the route."
The Teamsters they will all jump up in a most fretful way:
"Where is me boots? Where is me pants? Me socks is gone astray!"

At six o'clock it's breakfast and ev'ry man is out,
For ev'ry man who is not sick will sure be on the route,
There's sawyers and there's choppers to lay the timber low;
There's swampers and there's loggers to drag it to and fro.

And then comes up the logger, all at the break of day:
"Load up my slide, five hundred feet; to the river drive away." You
can hear those axes singing until the sun goes down. "Hurrah my
boys! The day is spent. To the shanty we are bound"

And when we reach the shanty, with cold hands and wet feet,
We there pull off our larrigans, our supper for to eat.
We sing and dance till nine o'clock; then to our bunks we climb.
Those winter months they won't be long in hurling down the pine.

The springtime rolls around at last, and then the boys will say:
"Heave down your saws and axes, boys and help to clear away."
And when the floating ice goes out, in business we will thrive:
Two hundred able- bodied men are wanted on the drive.

(AUTHOR ANONYMOUS)

CHAPTER 1

THE fury of the storm mounted. It rattled the windows of the small frame cottage in Ottawa's La Breton Flats, driving the snow against it in sheets. Meg and John Bains awoke before dawn and lay motionless in bed, watching the pale outline of the rafters above their heads.

The word of their father's death had come suddenly. The company office had sent a clerk with a curt note addressed to Meg and John's mother: "We learned today that your husband, Angus Bains, was killed in an accident. The body will arrive tomorrow. You must arrange burial." It was dated January 10, 1873, and signed Mr. R. J. Percy, President, Percy Lumber Company.

The full impact of their father's death had left a deep impression on the children. John was fourteen and Meg was a little over thirteen, but already they knew the hardships working people had to undergo. Now that their father was dead the prospects for their future looked bleaker still. How would their mother be able to make payments on their small cottage? How could any of the children continue with their schooling? It all seemed impossible.

Meg stirred restlessly. The image of the funeral the day before was foremost in her mind. Two spirited black Arabian horses pulled the sleigh-rigged hearse through the ice-bound streets. Behind shuffled the black-coated mourners, huddling into their clothes to keep out the biting wind that swept down out of the Algonquin Highlands to the west.

Among the mourners was a big hulking man by the name of Mr. Hardy, who was there representing the company. He was well over six feet, with sloping, deep-set shoulders and a heavy frame that gave a sense of restless power. His dark hair was shaggy, and the long mutton-chop sideburns and drooping moustache tried unsuccessfully to cover up the long, reddish scar that stood out on his cheek. Although he wore an expensive black suit, Hardy was obviously a man of the shanties and uncomfortable in city clothes.

After the funeral was over he had waited restlessly for the other neighbours and friends to go through the formal condolences that the manners of the age demanded, and then he approached Peggy Bains. Both Meg and John had noticed how their mother stiffened perceptibly.

"Mrs. Bains," he said without a hint of courtesy. "Mrs. Bains, I was talking to Mr. Percy, the company president, and he asked for you and your boy here to come and see him tomorrow. It's for nine A.M. sharp."

Their mother had eyed the man suspiciously. He was a company man, the foreman of the shanty where her husband had been killed, and she had learned long ago a man like this was to be treated warily. For some time she gave no reaction and then with a nod she curtly said, " I'll be there."

Meg lay in her warm bed, listening to the storm rage outside, wondering what that change had meant. She turned over, and in the pale light she could see that her brother was awake. "Psst!" she whispered. "John! John!"

Meg was sleeping with her younger sister, and John was with the two young boys, but they were separated by only a couple of feet. The older brother stirred. "Yes, what is it?"

"Who was that Mr. Hardy at the funeral?" She whispered, careful not to waken the younger children.

"He was the foreman of the shanty where father worked this season."

"Why did he ask you and mother to see Mr. Percy?"

"I don't know. Maybe he's going to give us a pension because father was killed."

Meg was quiet for a moment, pondering the answer. "I don't think so. Not from what dad used to say about the company."

"Well, maybe he will. That's all I said." John replied defensively.

They lay quietly in their beds for some time, staring into the dim light of the room.

Finally, Meg broke the silence. "What are we going to do, John? What can we do? We have to have money, or we won't be able to pay for the house and … " The prospects were so grim she was unable to finish the sentence.

John stared at the rafters for a long time until he was sure of what to tell his younger sister. "I've been thinking about it Meg," he said seriously. "In our family, whenever things got difficult, the men have always gone into the bush to get work. I'm fourteen years old now, and that's old enough to get a job and help support the family. When mother and I go to see Mr. Percy this morning I'm going to ask him for a job." In the 1870's most children were working by the age of fourteen, and some began when they were as young as ten.

Meg sat bolt upright in bed. "A job!" she said with surprise. "You can't take a job, you're too skinny and weak!"

"I am not skinny! It's just that I've never had a chance to work because mother wants us to study all the time."

"You couldn't work in a shanty, John Bains. Even I could do better because I'm stronger than you!"

"You are not stronger!"

"You're not going to go to the shanty and leave me behind, John. I can work harder than you ever could."

"Mr. Percy wouldn't let you go into the shanty 'cause you're a girl."

"What's that got to do with it?" Meg was indignant. "I can outwork anyone. Just ask mother. She'll tell you!"

"You can not. And anyway, there's no jobs for girls in the camps. Daddy told me they always need boys to help the cook and split wood and all those things but they never let girls into the shanties." John acted with the superiority of an older brother.

"Well, I can help the cook too."

"You can not. They won't let you go!"

"I'm going!" Meg insisted. "If you're going to go to shanty then you're not going to leave me behind."

"We'll see what mother says about that," John replied. "She won't let you go!" The sound of someone stirring in the kitchen had filtered up to the loft. It would be their mother beginning breakfast. "Let's go down and ask her. I bet she won't let you go." John concluded the argument with an air of certainty.

"All right, let's go," said Meg, leaping out of bed. They made their way down the steep stairs of the loft. In the kitchen, they found their mother slowly stirring the porridge that simmered on the wood cook stove. She was a big, square woman with strong arms and hands developed from years of hard work. Once again she seemed her calm, controlled self, as if she had coped with the emotional strain of her husband's sudden death.

Meg was the first into the kitchen and immediately began. "You're not going to let John go up to the shanty without me, are you mother? If he goes I can go too, can't I?"

"What's this?" said their mother, completely puzzled.

"It's John. He says he's going to go to Mr. Percy's and ask him for a job in the lumber camp and not take me along." Meg's excitement made the sentence completely confusing.

"Who's going to the shanty?" Peggy Bains, stared at her daughter, then turned to her son. "John, what's this all about?"

John felt sheepish. He had planned to have a serious talk with his mother before they went to see Mr. Percy, but now Meg had spoiled it. He tried as best he could to salvage the situation. "I've been thinking about it, mother," he said, uncertain of himself. "What with father being killed and everything, we won't have enough money to support the family, so when we go to see Mr. Percy I'm going to ask him for a job in one of the shanties."

"It's not fair," said Meg indignantly. "If John can go to work in the shanty then I should be allowed to go too!"

"Easy, children, easy," said their mother wearily. Under the tension of the argument, the strain of the last few days began to show. Not only did she have to withstand the shock of the death of her husband, and make the arrangements for the funeral, but now she had to decide how she was going to support her five young children without her husband. For the first time she felt desperately alone. Slowly she sat down at the kitchen table, as if to collect herself, and the children sat around her. "Now John," she said softly. "tell me again, what is this all about?"

"I want to go to shanty, mother. We've got to do something to get money now that father's dead. There are a lot of boys my age that are working. And father went to shanty when he was only fourteen. You have to stay here to look after the younger children and that leaves only me to go out and make money."

"And me too!" added Meg. "I can go to work in the shanty just as well as you."

"You can not. You're too young, and anyway you're a girl."

"Don't say that!" Meg was on her feet, angrily shouting. "Girls can work just as hard as boys, and I can work harder than you at any time!"

"Children! Children! Stop arguing right now!" The quiet of the kitchen was so sudden that they could hear the porridge bubbling on the stove and the wind of the storm rattling the windows.

Peggy Bains studied her hands for the longest time, and then looked up into the anxious faces of her two oldest children. They seemed so innocent, so unable to look after themselves. John was tall for his age, but his pale and delicate features made him seem almost fragile. And his weak soft hands had never held an axe or a heavy pole. Meg, sitting beside her, was shorter, though she seemed stronger in many ways than her brother. But how could she possibly leave home, a child barely thirteen?

What was the family to do? Her husband had been one of the best known shantymen in the Upper Ottawa River Valley. He was known by a thousand men in a hundred camps as one of the most skilled and resourceful men to ever go into a shanty, and he was making good wages because of it, but now he was dead. How could she ever hold onto the house? How could she keep the children in school? It all seemed so hopeless.

She began talking softly. "You don't understand. Your father and I wanted something different for you children. That's why you have been sent to school. You don't know the hardships of the shanties. The men work from well before dawn until long after dark at jobs that tire even the strongest of them."

"But I want to go, mother," pleaded John. "How else can you support the family?"

"We both want to go," added Meg.

"Please, children. I don't think you could do the work." But she sounded uncertain and indecisive.

"We'll go and see what Mr. Percy wants," said John. "And then I'll ask him for a job."

"No, *we'll* ask him," said Meg.

More in a desperate effort to stop the bickering than anything else, their mother finally agreed. "Yes, yes, all right! We'll all go and see Mr. Percy and then we'll decide what to do later." She smiled, breaking the tension of the argument. She felt proud of her two older children. They seemed so strong in the face of her own indecision.

John laughed suddenly, forgetting the argument of a moment before. "Come on Meg," he shouted. "We've got lots to do if we hope to get to Mr. Percy's before nine o'clock." The two scrambled upstairs laughing at each other. The other children were wakened, dressed, fed breakfast and then bundled up for school. For everyone the rough and tumble of family life was a welcome relief from the sober problems of the last few days.

CHAPTER 2

AN hour later, when the three of them went outside, they found the storm had already dumped six inches of snow on the city, and the dark heavy clouds promised even more. It blew across the roads and drifted around trees and the backs of houses. People struggled through the streets with their hats pulled down and collars turned up to keep the snow from blowing into their faces.

John and Meg were both dressed very poorly for such a storm. The custom dictated that the family must wear black to indicate they were in mourning, but neither of them had suitable clothes. John was wearing an old threadbare black mackinaw lent by a neighbour, and the black working pants of a friend. Meg wore a neighbour's heavy black shawl pulled across her shoulders. They hurried as fast as possible. It was a two-mile walk before they got to Percy's house, and the sooner out of the wind the better.

Ottawa was a city of contrasts. La Breton Flats, where the Bains family lived, was full of Scots, Irish and French Canadians who had streamed into the city in the decades between the 1830's and 50's looking for work. Those who were lucky owned or rented cottages cramped together on narrow pieces of land, but the poor lived in tenements stacked in long ugly rows along filthy back alleys. Most of the homes, even the poorest, were neat and tidy as the women tried to keep up the air of respectability despite the small wages their husbands brought home; some of the people, though, had finally lost hope in the face of impossible adversity, and their homes had deteriorated into rat-infested hovels.

There was another part of the city where the rich and powerful lived on their estates, pampered by servants and conveniences. They lived a gay life of parties and teas; sleigh rides during the winter on Dow's Lake, and steamboat rides in summer down the river to Montreal. A small group of families had made fabulous fortunes from timber, railways and land speculation, while others laboured twelve to fourteen hours a day for a dollar in wages.

Much of this variety of life was reflected in the scene as Meg, John and their mother walked to Mr. Percy's. At first, while they were still in La Breton Flats, they passed working men going off to their jobs and women going to do their shopping dressed in simple homespun clothing. Gradually, as they left the poorer section of the city, they began passing businessmen and government clerks dressed in heavy black coats made of the finest merino wool, and sober silk neckties. Finally they noticed sleighs pulled by fine Arabian horses and driven by servants dressed in grey suits and high button shoes. Inside were the faces of the wealthy aristocrats of the city on their way to their businesses or to social occasions, bundled up in fine cloaks, their knees draped with heavy buffalo robes.

There was much to see in this busy city, and John and Meg took in as much as possible. They passed the railway yards that had been completed in the 1860's to bring in the supplies to the lumbermen, and to haul the finely planed lumber to the markets in the United States. They went past the newly completed opera house, built to bring culture to the wealthy, and caught a glimpse of the new Parliament Buildings high on the embankment overlooking the river.

They were close to their destination, waiting at a corner for some carriages to pass, when Peggy Bains spoke loudly enough for Meg and John to hear. "Children," she said in her soft Ottawa Valley accent. "You'll not mention to Mr. Percy or Mr. Hardy or any of the others about the meetings that took place at our house last summer."

This seemed a strange request. John could not understand. "Why not?"

"It's just that it's best never to mention it to any of the company men. They might get inquisitive and then some of the other men might get into trouble."

"But I don't understand."

His mother smiled softly, her hand lightly resting on his shoulder. "Some day you'll understand well enough. It was all the talk about the union that went on. Some of it was illegal and the men could go to jail for it."

"Did dad do something against the law?" asked a surprised Meg.

Peggy Bains was an intense woman who expressed herself as precisely as she could and expected others to do the same. By the look she gave them both, the children knew they had all the information she would give on the subject.

The previous summer, Angus Bains had been home for almost four months. He had a job as a labourer on the widening of the Sapper's Bridge over the Ottawa River and was home every night. It had been a very special summer for the family. They went on outings together, and every evening Meg and John would talk to their father about a whole variety of things from life in the shanties to the trip on the rafts down to Quebec City.

But there were other things going on that summer. Every evening their small cottage was full with shantymen who talked seriously well into the night about the conditions of work in different shanties, rates of pay, safety conditions, quality of food and all sorts of other things. Often Meg and John would sit on the stairs leading up to the loft and listen to the men's stories of hardship and grief.

The children often asked why all these shantymen were coming to their house, but they got only vague answers to their questions. They assumed the reason was that they were too young to be told — but maybe the real reason, after what their mother said, was that their father was involved in some illegal activity. John wanted to question his mother further, but they arrived at Mr. Percy's estate and other things distracted them.

A tall wrought iron fence surrounded the estate, and they had to walk around it until they found the heavy gates that were locked tight against intruders. Meg rang the bell, and the three of them waited nervously to be let in. The house was a large, cut-stone, three-storey mansion, trimmed in perfect white. Six large pillars held up the roof of the spacious porch of the entranceway. The grounds were huge, with full spruce trees of different varieties scattered about on the lawn, and behind the house was a complex of stables that housed the horses and carriages that took the Percy family around to their various social engagements.

Meg was particularly nervous about the meeting, wishing all of a sudden she was far away from that spot, but she had insisted on coming and there was no backing out now. Impulsively she reached up and rang the bell again.

"That's enough, there! That's enough!" shouted a manservant coming to the gate. "Do you think you are his Lordship himself?" The man was clearly annoyed to find three shabbily dressed people at the gate. Peggy Bains had to explain in detail why they were there before the man would let them in, but finally the gate swung open.

The three of them walked up the neatly shovelled pathway towards the front doors, and suddenly the servant was shouting at them again. "Where do you think you're going?" They turned around in puzzlement. "Don't you know that that door's used by your betters. The likes of you go around to the service entrance at the back where you belong." He said it in a sharp way, as if talking to ignorant people.

Peggy Bains muttered something under her breath, but the three of them obediently followed the order. At the back door they again explained who they were to the maid. She disappeared, leaving them standing in the draughty, unheated back hallway for what seemed like hours. It was a humbling feeling. Meg became more and more anxious, and twisted her mittened hands back and forth. John stamped his feet and tried to make his baggy unkempt clothes appear more presentable. Only their mother appeared calm, but inwardly she felt a simmering resentment.

Finally the maid returned. "Right this way. Hurry now, please. Mr. Percy and Mr. Hardy are busy men." The maid showed them where to leave their snow-dampened coats and overshoes, and then led the way through the kitchen and hallways, leaving the three of them to hurry behind.

The richness and opulence was even more apparent inside the house. Indian rugs made of silk muffled the sound of their feet. The doors were made of the finest oak, and some of the walls and bannisters bore richly carved wood panels. Crystal gaslamps lighted the rooms, showing several oil paintings. It would have taken a whole season of the hardest labour in one of Percy's shanties before Angus Bains would earn enough to buy even the smallest of the Indian rugs that were scattered about on the floor, but one season's profits of Mr. Percy's company were enough to buy this whole estate. He was one of the biggest lumber barons in the Ottawa Valley, and he lived in this magnificent house to prove it to everyone.

The maid stopped at a large set of doors and knocked. "Come in," said a voice, and they found themselves in a large study. Light streamed into the room through the enormous French doors that led into the garden. On one wall was a huge fireplace stacked high with large pieces of burning coal, and another was covered with books and paintings. At the far end, near the fireplace, was a large oak desk with two people sitting behind it.

The larger of the two men was Hardy. He seemed bigger and more impressive physically than he had at the funeral the day before, but he looked uncomfortable and out of place. Hardy was a man in his late thirties, with brown hair beginning to turn slightly grey. His eyes searched restlessly from face to face, as if instinctively looking for the slightest weakness in his opponents standing on the opposite side of the desk. His shoulders were slightly stooped and his arms were folded, but his hands clenched and unclenched restlessly, showing his inner tension.

Only Mr. Percy felt completely at home in this room. He was a small man in his early fifties who had grown fat from inactivity. For a couple of seasons he had gone into the shanties, but that was long ago, and it had left no mark on him. His hands were pink and soft and his face pale; his hair and moustache were neatly barbered, for he had been freshly shaved and perfumed only a short while before. The black morning coat that he wore was matched with a wing-collared shirt and an ascot tie with a diamond stickpin. He spoke rapidly in a high-pitched voice, oozing confidence.

John, Meg and their mother pressed forward to stand in front of the desk, like children ready to be reprimanded by their superiors. They were not invited to sit down or to make themselves comfortable.

Mr. Percy cleared his throat, folded his hands over his large stomach and took command of the interview. "Mr. Hardy, is this the family of the man that was killed in your Cache Lake shanty?"

"Yes sir. But … but I invited Mrs. Bains and her son. Not this young girl." Hardy's discomfort was apparent.

"This is my daughter Meg," Peggy Bains explained. "She is old enough to be involved in the family decisions."

"I see." Percy paused, playing with the gold chain on his pocket watch. "Anyway, Mrs. Bains, I have a notion that I will offer a job to your young son here … have him work up in the shanty. Would you like that, boy?"

This was a surprise. John had intended to ask for a job and here it was being offered to him. "Yes sir, I certainly would, sir. Thank you very much, sir," he said eagerly.

"Do you think you're worthy, boy?"

"Worthy, sir?" John was uncertain what he meant.

"Can you work hard, boy? That's what I mean." Percy leaned forward and pointed a finger at John. "I won't have any laggers in my shanties. Work all my men hard. It's good for them. I can't stand men who are lazy. Would you be lazy if I gave you a job?"

"No, sir," said the boy anxiously. "No, sir, I need the job and I'll work hard, sir. You'll see. It's important to me because I have to support my mother and family."

Meg suddenly interrupted the interview. A sense of stubborn determination marked the tone of her voice. "I want to go and work in the shanty too, Mr. Percy!"

Percy was surprised. "What's that you say?"

"I want to go and work in the shanty. It's only fair that if you let my brother go I should go too."

"What am I going to use a young girl for?"

"You'll see, Mr. Percy. I can work hard. I'm just as strong as my brother, and I help around the house all the time. It's only fair to let me have a chance of helping my mother just like John."

A smile crossed Percy's face as he stroked his chin, considering the possibilities. The timber trade, like most industries in the nineteenth century, depended on child labour to do many of the menial jobs. In the shanties, most of the camp jobs were done by boys, but maybe there would be a possibility of using a girl.

Meg was so anxious to give a good impression that she blurted on, trying as hard as possible to be convincing. "I can wash dishes, and I can make beds. I bet I can even split wood and look after horses. And I can do other things too — you'll see. Like maybe chopping down trees. Things like that. You won't regret hiring me, Mr. Percy."

All the time Meg was talking, John looked at her angrily. This outburst might lose him the chance for the job. Why was she always doing these things?

But Mr. Percy seemed only amused. "What do you think, Mr. Hardy?" He said turning to the big foreman. "We have a woman who's the cook up in that shanty, Mrs. Ferguson, and we've had trouble keeping camp boys. Maybe if we kept the two children one could help the men in the bush?"

Hardy stirred his shoulders restlessly, fiddling with the sheet of papers on his knee. He seemed disturbed, uncertain of himself. "Ah, Mr. Percy. I don't like this at all." He said it in a low tone of voice, as if he wished the others couldn't hear.

"Don't like what, Hardy?"

"Them coming to my shanty. I don't like it."

"Why not?" Mr. Percy seemed genuinely puzzled.

"It's just that … ah … " He searched for a reason. "Maybe they wouldn't be strong enough."

"Aye, they do look weak, and young too." Mr. Percy seemed to be reconsidering.

"No, I'm strong, sir. You'll see," John said anxiously.

"I am too," added Meg. "I can work as hard as anyone."

"It isn't that Mr. Percy. It's just that I'm afraid of trouble, and … " His voice trailed off.

John was desperate. The family needed this job. "You'll see, Mr. Percy. I can do the work. I'm really strong, and I won't be any trouble to you or anyone else."

Meg was nodding in agreement. "That's true with me too."

Percy leaned back into his chair, his hands folded across his large stomach. "I must say I like the eagerness the two of you show. It shows that you'll listen to orders. But Mr. Hardy is right. We've had some bad trouble up in that shanty, and I won't put up with any more of it. All this talk about the union and strikes. I won't have it. I will have the police in there if I must, but I will have order and discipline in my shanties."

"I won't cause trouble, sir. You'll see." John pleaded.

"That's good. That's the right attitude to have." Percy was quiet for a moment, pondering his decision. "Mr. Hardy, I can understand your concern, and I agree with it, but I must say that we have some obligation to this family. The men must know that if they get hurt or killed we will help look after their families. It's the code of the shanties and we'd be hard pressed to break it."

Hardy folded his arms and shifted in his chair. His eyes darted from person to person. Finally, he nodded his head in agreement, but it was obvious he did not like these developments.

"We agree, then, Mr. Hardy, that we hire these two children." Hardy nodded reluctantly. "It's settled, but let me tell the two of you that if you fall in with those unionists and cause us any trouble we will make so much trouble for you that you'll wish that you'd never heard of a union. Is that understood?"

John and Meg were anxious to please, and nodded eagerly.

"Mr. Hardy will be in the camp to see that you do. He has a few things to clean up here, but he'll watch every movement of the two of you for the rest of the season. So I want you to work hard and listen to him. Do you understand?"

"Yes sir," said John.

Percy paused for a moment organizing his thoughts. "Now, for the arrangements. There is a teamster hauling supplies into camp. He leaves the day after tomorrow from our warehouse in Renfrew. The two of you will go up there tomorrow afternoon by train to meet him. It'll take you longer to get to the camp with him than if you went with Mr. Hardy, but maybe you can be of help to the teamster on the way. Come here this afternoon and my accountant will have the train tickets ready." Percy paused again. "Oh yes and another thing. We'll pay the boy fifty cents a day and the young girl twenty-five cents, plus room and board. The money will come to you every week, Mrs. Bains."

Peggy Bains had said virtually nothing since coming into the room. Now, standing stiffly in front of the desk, she calmly stared at Percy without a hint of emotion on her face, and addressed him with quiet determination.

"Mr. Percy you offer us seventy-five cents a day for the employment of my two children. I don't even want them to go to the shanty. They are too young to face the hardships of that place. I need a pension from you. That is only fair. My husband was killed while in your employment. I see it as your responsibility to support my family until they finish their schooling. That is only justice."

For a moment there was silence. Both Percy and Hardy seemed to be stunned by this show of forcefulness. Then Percy exploded. "Who do you think you are, madam? Have you no respect? I am the owner of this company. Your husband was killed through his own stupidity! I cannot pay for that!"

"Was it an accident, or what happened? I would like to know."

Hardy was suddenly on his feet. "I tell you she's a troublemaker just like her husband. They'd like to run the shanty." The quickness of Hardy's anger surprised everyone. His face was a deep red, and there seemed almost a touch of uncontrolled madness in his sudden explosion.

Percy soothed him. "It's all right, Hardy. It's all right. I'll handle it." For a moment the room was deathly quiet, with all eyes on Hardy as he struggled to bring his anger under control. Then Percy started again. "Now what is this, Mrs. Bains? Are you saying that someone is responsible for your husband's death?"

"I don't know, Mr. Percy. Perhaps I'll never know, but one thing is certain, and that is that seventy-five cents a day for the labour of my two children does not compensate me for my husband's death."

Percy was incensed. "This is unspeakable. Here I give your children good jobs and you ask for more. Let me tell you I do not give out charity to able-bodied people, madam. You can look after yourself."

Peggy Bains did not back down. She showed no hint of emotion. "I do not ask for charity, Mr. Percy. I ask only for justice. My husband was killed while working for you, but instead of meeting your responsibilities you want to take my two young children, and still give me half the income my husband received. I ask for justice, that is all." Her feet were planted firmly on the rug. She looked proud and defiant.

Percy was angry, but still controlled the situation. "I'll not have this from the likes of you, madam! Your husband must have been one of the ones causing trouble in that shanty. Get out, and take your children too! I've seen your kind before. You'll be demanding more and more, but you'll get none of it from me!"

Peggy Bains turned and started walking out of the study. She knew she had lost, but it was still a moral victory to be able to tell Percy what she thought of his offer right in the comfort of his own study. Meg followed her mother. She was not certain of all of the reasons for the argument, but she felt she had to protect and comfort her mother against any further attacks by Percy.

But John stood his ground, watching them leave. He could not understand his mother. She was ruining the family's only chance for support. They would be destitute without some kind of income. The house would be lost, the children would be scattered to orphanages, and their mother would be forced into the home for the poor. He had to stay. "Mr. Percy, Mr. Percy, I'll take the job, sir!"

For a moment Percy said nothing, but then he collected himself and seemed to consider John's statement. "I don't know, boy. It seems to me that if you're like your mother then you're going to be a troublemaker."

"No sir, no really I won't! It's just that my mother's upset. That's all."

Percy leaned across the desk and wagged a short pudgy finger at John. "You listen to me, boy. If I give this job to you and your sister I don't want any trouble. Do you understand? I want you to be obedient to Hardy."

"Yes sir! We will, sir!"

"Because I'm fed up with trouble in that shanty. What with the men trying to take over and all … I'll have none of it. Do you understand?" He was shouting now. "If I have to I'll get each and every one of them. I'm going up there in the spring, and if there's been any trouble, any trouble at all, I'll have men in jail. Do you understand?" He thumped the desk for emphasis. "If you or your sister have anything to do with the union, boy, I'll have the police on your tail so quick it'll make your head spin!" And he thumped the desk again.

"Yes sir, I understand, sir!"
"All right, then the jobs are yours."

CHAPTER 3

EARLY the next morning, the two excited children took leave of their family and travelled north on the new railway to Renfrew, some fifty miles up the Ottawa River. They asked directions until they found the company warehouse, where they presented themselves to the foreman and gave him a note from Mr. Percy. The two were put to work immediately, helping to load the sleigh that they were to take to the Algonquin Highlands the next day.

The sleigh was huge, almost twenty feet long and over eight feet wide, and it was being loaded high above the sides with enormous hogsheads, or barrels of salt pork, and hundred-pound bags of flour and dried beans. Meg and John were eager to show their worth, and they struggled to get the sacks of flour into the back of the sleigh. Even with one on each side the only thing they accomplished was to burn their hands raw on the rough material. They marvelled at the strength of O'Riley, the teamster they were to travel with, who could swing the sacks onto the back of the sleigh in one easy motion, and hoist the enormous hogsheads up to the edge and then roll them into place. By the end of that first night they were so tired they fell asleep in the hayloft right after supper and slept like the dead.

At six the next morning, O'Riley roused them out of their sleep. He had brought them a breakfast of salt pork, bread and cold tea, and although the two children could barely stomach the cold salty meat they forced it down without a word, knowing full well that on this trip they would have to eat whenever they got a chance. After breakfast they joined the teamster to help harness the huge Clydesdale horses that would haul the sleigh into the highlands.

Both Meg and John watched how O'Riley rigged the harnesses. They had never harnessed a horse before and they knew that they would have to learn quickly to be of any use on the trip. The teamster was a short, powerfully built man whose body rippled with tight, hard muscles that he had developed from constant hard physical work. Like a lot of working men, he was a good teacher. His good-humoured, relaxed manner made both the children like him immediately. Meg particularly felt warm about him because he treated them with a sense of rough equality rather than giving her favours because she was a girl. He knew that if she was ever to be accepted in the shanty she would have to pull her weight from the very beginning.

Finally, the horses were ready. They backed them into their traces and shackled into position; then they pulled the sleigh out of the large warehouse. Dawn had greyed the sky in the east as they drove through the sleeping village, and by the time they got out into the countryside the sun was up on a cold clear day. The horses walked in an easy rhythm, making the sleigh runners sing as they crunched through the cold, hard-packed snow.

John and Meg sat high up on the sleigh beside the teamster, watching the scene unfold before them. To the north they could still see the Bonnechere River winding its way through the town, and beyond that lay gentle hills. In the south the sun shone on dark green ridges that marked the watershed between the Madawaska and the Bonnechere rivers. To the west, directly before them, was a series of hills that would gradually grow in elevation until they became the Algonquin Highlands some ninety miles in the distance.

O'Riley explained to them that it was crucial to the life of the shanties that trips such as these get through. The supplies could be hauled only during a very short period when the snow gave a good ground cover and the ice on the lakes was strong enough to carry the weight of the sleighs. All activities in the timber trade were geared around the seasons. In the fall the trains from Chicago arrived full of the hogsheads of salt pork. During the summer the company purchasing agents were all over the valley buying up flour and beans. Through the fall and early winter the warehouses of the companies filled up, and then in January began the frantic hauling of supplies with the hope that they could get enough into the shanties by the end of March to satisfy their needs for the rest of the season and the beginning of the next.

Renfrew was the start of the hauling into the shanties in the headwaters of the Madawaska River system, because it was the end of the railway and the start of the Opeongo Line. In 1856 the road had been cut through by the government to encourage settlement in that area of the country. Now, seventeen years later, the road, or at least the first part of it, was wide enough for two sleighs to pass.

In their first day of travelling they made good time. The road was hard-packed from the pounding it received from many teams, and they were able to make eighteen miles to a small collection of buildings called Dacre. On the second day it ran for about nine miles along the foot of St. Patrick Fault and they began a long steep climb up Plaunt's Mountain. The climb took so much out of the horses that once they were at the top the teamster blanketed his animals, tied on feed bags of oats and let them rest for half an hour. From that point on, the Opeongo Line was less well used. The snow often drifted in, making the runners of the sleigh sink deeply and creating an extra drag for the horses to pull. Often the three of them had to put on snowshoes and walk in front of the team, helping to pack down the snow.

On the evening of the second day out of Renfrew, they stayed at a small inn on the Opeongo Line called Clontarf. After supper some of the local farmers gathered to talk to their neighbours and sip drams of whisky. They seemed tired, defeated men who could talk about little more than the hardships they faced in trying to wrest a living out of the infertile soil.

But John and Meg were too exhausted to listen for long. They climbed into the loft, found a straw mattress, and with barely a word to each other went to sleep. The next morning they were covered with bites from the bedbugs that infested the mattress. In spite of their condition neither of them complained. It was as if there was a pact between them that together they could defeat any hardships.

During the day when they were on the sleigh, they talked to pass the time. Even though O'Riley had known the children's father he was reluctant to talk to them about him until he knew them better. It was the morning of the third day before he began. He drifted from issue to issue in a singsong voice.

"Angus Bains was one of the best shantymen on the Madawaska, and a finer man you wouldn't want to work with. He brought the men together like no one else I knew. Before Bains, the Irish and the French and the Scots used to fight all the time, every man in the camp picking the side of his countrymen no matter what was the justice of the issue. But your father made them see that this was just dividing them, that if they fought over little things they'd never join together over the big ones. He was right too. The union could be a real power if all the men stood behind it. The owners have vowed to break it, but for the men the union's their only salvation."

It was John who was most concerned about the union. "But do you think it'd be a good thing, O'Riley?"

"It's hard to tell, boy. Depends on a lot of things."

"But, what's the union for? I don't understand."

"You don't know, boy, after your father did so much?"

"He never talked to us about it."

The teamster was quiet for a long time. "Well it's like this," he began. "The conditions in some of the shanties are bad. The food is bad, and the wages are bad, and the foremen drive the men all the time. They are tired of it and say they need a union of some kind to bargain for them."

"But the union's illegal, isn't it?" said John, pressing the point in an effort to understand.

"The company men will tell you that, but it seems to me there's nothing wrong with organizing a union or any group. All I know is that conditions are bad and the men see that a union is their only chance."

John was quiet for almost a minute, trying to understand the issue. "How can we oppose the company?" he finally said. "Percy told us that he'd put any man in jail who organized a union against him. Isn't it our job to obey the bosses?"

"Don't be silly, John" said Meg, interrupting the discussion. "Dad took part in the union. It must be the right thing for the shantymen."

"But Percy said it was illegal, Meg!"

"Don't be so scared. You know dad supported it so it must be all right."

"I'm not scared! It's just that I've got to do the right thing!" John became quiet, but somehow he was still not convinced.

They travelled in silence for some time, each watching the scenery of the Opeongo Line, buried in their own thoughts. Finally Meg asked O'Riley the question that had been bothering her. "How was dad killed, O'Riley? Do you know anything about it?"

The teamster shifted in his seat and studied the shanks of his horses for a long time before he answered. "It's hard to know. They say that he was struck by a tree that twisted as it fell. At least that's what they told me." He was quiet for a moment. "I was the one who brought the body down on my last trip. I saw the wound and I've thought about it often since. He died from a blow on the left side of his head. I looked at the body carefully because I was curious, and all I could see was that one wound." He paused again fingering his black beard thoughtfully. "Now it would seem to me that if a man was killed by a falling tree it might hit him on the head, but it would also catch him on the chest or on the arms or legs or somewhere. But not with your father. There was one wound on the left side of the head and no other."

"Do you think he was killed on purpose?" Meg asked anxiously.

"I dunno. I'm not a doctor, but the wound could have been made by an axe just as easy as a tree."

"You must mean that someone killed him."

"I don't know any more than what I told you. I say this only because you are the children of Angus Bains and have a right to know what I saw, but I know nothing more."

"But you must know something else." Meg pleaded.

No matter how many questions that were put to him O'Riley would say no more. Both Meg and John felt a growing uneasiness about their father's death. Maybe there would be some simple explanations to all of these questions, but now there was only nagging doubt, and the closer they got to the Algonquin Highlands the greater the mystery seemed to grow.

That night they slept at a stopping place called Brudenell, the fourth night they were at Hopefield and the fifth at Barry's Bay. They were making no more than ten miles a day, and on some days less than eight, even though they were on the trail from sun up to sun down. The horses had to haul the heavily laden sleigh up enormously long hills and ease it downhill with the weight pressing against their haunches. The country was so wild that they rarely saw a farm and seldom came across people.

When they set out from Barry's Bay on the sixth day, the Opeongo Line went west for another three miles and then turned north. The teamster left the road at that point and struck southwest over a rough tote road for about two miles until they came to the shore of Bark Lake. Without hesitation he steered his team out onto the ice and started heading south down a long inlet. It was good to be out of the bush for a change and to be able to see long distances. They were deep into the highlands now, surrounded by dark green forbidding hills that rose steeply out of the lake for almost a thousand feet. They could see for miles, and everywhere they looked was wilderness without the mark of man.

In many places the ice was blown free of snow, and they were able to move the horses at a fast walk. They went about two miles due south down the inlet until they came to the main part of the lake. Then they turned northwest and worked their way up to the end of the lake. There they found a small collection of log buildings called Shannon's Stopping Place, where they had a miserable cold supper of rolled oats and stale bread, and spent another night on vermin-infested straw mattresses.

The next morning it was a welcome relief to get back on the trail again. Now that they were away from the Opeongo Line it had become little more than a trail through the bush marked by axe slashes on the trees. They travelled all day along the tops of hills down into ravines and up the other side. The going was difficult for the horses, and the three of them walked most of the way in front of the team with their snowshoes on to help tramp down the trail. It was bitterly cold, with a chilling wind that struck them whenever they were on a hilltop or in open spaces. Late in the afternoon, with the sun close to setting, they began coming down a long hill that stretched for almost half a mile before they broke into a clearing and found a couple of fields and a few log buildings that made up the Whitney Stopping Place.

John and Meg helped bed down the horses for the night. Their own exhaustion was so great that when they finally came into the rough log hut they could do little more than collapse on the floor next to the fireplace. After a couple of minutes' rest Meg got up. "Come on, John, we need to get our supper."

"I'm not hungry Meg. I'm just going to sit here a little longer." Exhaustion marked his face.

"We've got to eat to keep up our strength."

"Just let me be for a little longer. I'll be all right."

At home John had spent most of his time on his studies. He was less prepared for the hardships of the trail than his younger sister.

"Please, John," Meg pleaded. "We've got to eat to keep up our strength."

"Leave me alone." The boy said with sudden annoyance. "I don't need you to tell me what to do."

"But you've got to eat, John!"

O'Riley was close by and overheard the exchange. "Come on, lad. Up you get. All the shantymen have to eat to survive."

John struggled to his feet, annoyed with himself for letting the others see his exhaustion. After a supper of beans, pork and tea, he and Meg found their beds and fell asleep immediately.

It was scarcely five-thirty the next morning when O'Riley shook them awake. They harnessed the horses with numbed fingers, ate a hurried breakfast and led the team and the heavily laden sleigh out onto the frozen Galeairy Lake. They travelled due west across the lake into a brisk wind for most of the morning, until they came to a narrows in the lake. There the teamster left the ice and took the sleigh over a twisting trail that went over a small ridge beside the lake. For almost two hours the horses laboured over the trail. There was the slight possibility that the ice might be rotten, and O'Riley was too good a teamster to take unnecessary risks.

Once they got back onto the ice again, the horses kept up a steady pace and within an hour they were at the extreme west end of the lake. There they found a short trail that took them from Galeairy Lake up about 350 yards to Rock Lake. The trail bypassed a set of rapids that was kept open by the current and they could see the log chute that had been built a few seasons before to take the timber past the broken water on the spring drive. Finally, not long before nightfall, after travelling another two miles up Rock Lake, they came to a small stopping place where they spent the night. After supper O'Riley told them to get a good night's rest. "You'll need it," he said. "Tomorrow will be the roughest day yet."

He was true to his word. They were deep into the highlands now and the country was more rugged than anything they had been through. High hills rose directly out of the ice-covered lake. Often they could see the reddish granite rock of exposed cliffs. The streams were torrents of water that in places flowed so quickly they did not freeze even in midwinter. The snow was four feet deep, and every step of the way the three of them had to break the trail. The horses were already close to exhaustion from the long trip, but now they had to wade through snow that was knee and sometimes chest-deep.

The tote road they travelled was not a road at all. A few trees had been cut to let a large sleigh pass, and slashes had been made on the trees to mark the way, but no more had been done. That day was unending. Heavy snow had fallen since the last team had come this way, and a number of trees had to be cleared from the path to get the sleigh through. But O'Riley forced the pace, returning again and again to prod the horses as they floundered in the deep drifts. On they moved, slowly, with only short breaks to let the horses catch their breath; and the further they struggled the deeper they went into this wild country of rock and snow and trees.

Both John and Meg felt a growing exhaustion. Towards late afternoon John, in particular, was feeling that all he wanted to do was find a place to sleep, but he knew O'Riley could not let him rest. He forced himself to put one snowshoe in front of the other, and finally, just when he thought he could not carry on any more, they came into a small clearing and found a stopping place set down on the shores of Lawrence Lake.

CHAPTER 4

THE next morning was the tenth day on the trail without a break and it was to be the last. In spite of their exhaustion they were again up before dawn, harnessing the horses for the last eight-mile push into the shanty at Cache Lake. The weather was threatening: dark clouds covered the sky, a brisk wind came out of the northeast and it seemed as if any minute snowflakes would begin to fall. O'Riley talked to the manager of the stopping place, and they agreed that all the signs pointed to bad weather, but still the teamster decided to take the chance.

The tote road led them up to a ridge and followed the crest of the hills a number of miles. It had been several days since anyone had travelled the road, and the fresh snow had to be packed down every step of the way. By mid-morning a light snow was beginning to fall out of a heavy overcast sky. It took them until noon before they slowly came down a hill and broke out onto the ice at Harness Lake. Another half-mile further north and they could see a collection of buildings that had been the camp the men of the Percy Company had lived in the previous season.

As the sleigh came across the ice, O'Riley turned to the children sitting on either side of him and smiled good-naturedly. "We'll take the rest of the day off. Looks like the weather could close in and it's too risky to take a chance to go further. We can go the rest of the way tomorrow."

The thought of having the afternoon to themselves to rest and do anything they wanted was a wish come true. But suddenly O'Riley said, "Smoke! Someone's at the shanty."

When they pulled up two men came out of the building to meet them. One was called Adams, an old company shantyman, and the other was MacInnes, the camp shanty clerk who did all the book-work for the Percy Lumber Company on this Limit.

O'Riley climbed down from the rig. "Unshackle the horses, kids. Take them into the stables and give them a rub down." Then the teamster went to meet the other two men.

Meg and John went about their work until they overheard an argument breaking out. "I tell you, MacInnes," O'Riley was saying angrily, "My horses are just too tired to go any further. It's another four miles on to the shanty and the snow's already begun. Chances are we wouldn't make it before nightfall."

The two children stopped to listen. MacInnes was a small man, scarcely over five feet tall, with a ruddy complexion and reddish hair curling out from under his black-brimmed hat. He had come to Canada from his native Scotland three years before, and although he had lived most of that time in various lumber camps, he was a clerk and not a shantyman, and had little knowledge of the ways of the bush. But that did not make him less stubborn. "I tell you," he said, "I came over this morning with Adams, here, and we made the walk in little more than an hour. My work is finished, and I need to get back to Cache Lake. Surely we can travel the four miles in what's left of the daylight."

O'Riley was clearly annoyed. "This tote road's in bad condition. My animals are exhausted from the trip. Those two youngsters are tired and I'm tired, and even the weather's closing in. It's too risky. We'll spend the night here and go in the morning."

"Don't be stupid. We need to go back now," insisted MacInnes in his high-pitched voice.

O'Riley was angry. "If you want to go back then go back on snowshoes the way you came. But I tell you I don't want to get stuck in the bush overnight."

"You're like all the rest around here," shouted Mac-Innes. "You want to sit around all day and do nothing. Well, you'll not do it with me around. I'll have you respect me and the company, or you'll not have a job any longer."

For a moment the two stared angrily at each other, neither willing to back down; then the teamster laughed. "You think you know everything there is to know about this country, MacInnes. Well then, we'll go on if that's what your worship wants, and we'll see what happens." He strode over to the sleigh, his face red and his mittened hands clenching into fists. "Shackle those horses up again. We'll show the shanty clerk his tote roads."

Adams had more work to do at the Harness Lake shanty, and he would stay overnight. He prepared them a quick lunch while O'Riley gave the team a light feed of oats and a little water. When they finished eating, John and Meg pulled the heavy blankets off the horses, the four of them climbed aboard, and with a crack of the reins the two exhausted animals pulled the sleigh back onto the ice of Harness Lake.

When they got to the other side of the lake, John, Meg and the teamster got out, put on their snowshoes and went in front to break trail. O'Riley led his horses with the reins in his hands, while John and Meg walked in front carrying axes ready to clear away any fallen trees or branches. The shanty clerk sat up on the sleigh, watching the three of them without lifting a hand to help. He was a company man, and in his view only the shantymen did the manual work.

The trail was worse than any they had been on. Over and over again the horses got bogged down, but with prodding they would struggle and pull at their traces until once again the sleigh moved. Coming off the lake they had to climb a steep hill that drained the animals' energy, but finally they got to the top, and the teamster let them rest for a few minutes.

The snow was coming down so hard by now that they could see no more than thirty yards ahead of them. There was little more than an hour's daylight left. When they began again the tote road led them along the crest of a series of ridges generally in a northwest direction. With the twilight lengthening the shadows and the heavy snow drifting through the trees it was increasingly difficult to see the trail.

O'Riley was concentrating on his team, trying to draw every last ounce of strength out of them, and he was not watching closely enough. Suddenly, before he could do anything, the horses waded neck-deep into a hole and the sleigh skidded in behind them.

"Hey teamster, what are you doing?" Shouted Mac-Innes from on top of the sleigh.

O'Riley became furious. "You'll be silent, Mac-Innes, or I'll make you silent!" His fist waved threateningly at the shanty clerk.

For an instant tempers were close to the boiling point, but then both men realized that the situation was far too serious to take time to argue. O'Riley could not resist getting in the last word: "Let this show you, Mac-Innes. In this country the risks are too great. When men and horses are tired they should rest, or something like this happens almost every time." The shanty clerk said nothing in reply.

It took thirty precious minutes to get the horses and sleigh out. O'Riley, John and Meg had to climb into the hole and unshackle the animals from their traces. Once they had led them away, the three of them had to turn the front runners by hand until they pointed uphill. Then the horses had to be backed into the traces again and with a massive lift they lurched the sleigh out of the hole and back onto level ground.

When they were finished it was dark in the bush, and the snowstorm cut the visibility to virtually nothing. O'Riley found a lantern in the back of the sleigh, and finally on the third match he got the coal oil lit. John and Meg went ahead with the light, looking for the blazes on the trees marking the trail. O'Riley led his horses and MacInnes climbed back up onto the sleigh.

John held the lantern high above his head, and Meg walked beside him searching for the blazes. Both were exhausted, but John was at the point where he could do little more than place one snowshoe in front of the other, knowing they had to keep to the trail or become hopelessly lost for the rest of the night. Suddenly, he stumbled and fell headlong into the snow. He struggled to his feet with Meg's help.

"Are you all right, John?" she asked anxiously.

"Yes, yes, fine." But it was as if he was in a trance.

They started again, plodding step after weary step. John's feet felt as if they were disconnected from his body. He tried to remember to look for the axe slashes on the trees, but he was more and more in a dream. The next he knew, he had tripped over his snowshoes and was lying face down in the snow.

Meg was crying. "John, John, get up please, John!" She pulled him out of the snow, the tears streaming down her face.

O'Riley was beside them. In the light of the lantern their faces showed concern. "MacInnes! MacInnes!" The teamster shouted. "Get off that sleigh. These children are exhausted!"

"Why?" said the shanty clerk, indignant that he might be forced to walk.

Meg screamed at him. "I hate you, Mr. MacInnes, I hate you! If anything happens to my brother I'll blame you for it." Her tears were mixed with her anger.

MacInnes scrambled down in the face of the opposition. O'Riley lifted the boy onto the seat of the sleigh and then Meg climbed up beside him.

"You must stay awake, John," O'Riley said. "And Meg, you must see to it that he stays awake. Otherwise he will freeze. The two of you are to stamp your feet and clap your hands to keep the circulation going. Do you understand?"

Meg nodded, but John still seemed groggy. O'Riley grabbed him by the front of the coat and shook him. "Listen to me! You must stay awake and keep moving! Do you understand?"

"Yes, yes, O'Riley. I'll do it. I'm awake now."

The teamster left and went to the front of his team. "Damn you, MacInnes. If anything happens to either of those children I'll have your hide." The shanty clerk said nothing to defend himself.

They started again. MacInnes was in front with the lantern, searching for the slashes, O'Riley led the team, and Meg cradled her brother on the sleigh.

"Stay awake, John. Please stay awake," she pleaded with him. "Move your hands and your feet," she repeated over and over again.

They travelled on at a snail's pace through the pitch-black bush for what seemed like hours. The lantern bobbed up ahead. O'Riley struggled with his exhausted team, forcing them on with an iron will, and the children struggled to stay awake.

Suddenly, there was a bone-chilling howl. The horses' ears stood up, and one neighed in a frightened way. Everyone froze where they were. Then there was another howl, and several yips. O'Riley struggled with his spooked team until he finally brought them under control. "Wolves," he shouted. "We have to press on!"

They continued their procession. They were going down a steep hill now, and the sleigh slid forward, pressing its full weight onto the horses' haunches. O'Riley had to turn and twist the sleigh back and forth to keep to the grade. He walked between his two huge animals, trying to talk them out of their fear of wolves, and calming them enough to carry the immense weight down the steep incline in spite of their exhaustion. At one point the sleigh tilted dangerously over. There was a fear that the load might shift and crash over the side, but O'Riley forced his animals on until gradually it righted itself.

There was another howl close by. One of the horses tossed its head with such violence that it pulled O'Riley off balance. There was a tense moment as he struggled to bring them under control, then a long pause while he coaxed the frightened team once more. Then, gradually, he began moving them one foot at a time down the treacherous tote road. They proceeded slowly, twisting back and forth, guiding the sleigh with every step. Finally, the hill seemed to level out. A few steps more and they were on the ice of Cache Lake.

They paused for a moment to let the tension ease away. The snow had stopped, the heavy dark clouds had disappeared, and in the east a sliver of a moon had just risen above the hills, casting a pale eerie light over the scene. The flat white lake stood in contrast against the dark rounded hills that rose hundreds of feet from the lake's surface. Around them the wind stirred the pine trees restlessly. Somewhere, far off in the distance, they could still hear the yips and howls of the wolf pack on the hunt.

"How are you, John?" Meg asked.

The rest in the sleigh had made the boy feel much better, and suddenly his dignity was hurt by his younger sister's mothering. "I'm just fine," he said with annoyance. "Who do you think you are, trying to look after me? Just stop it!"

"I was just trying to help."

O'Riley started to laugh. The remark seemed in such contrast to the danger they had faced only moments before that he could not contain himself. Between laughs he said, "You've done well, John. Both of you have done well. You'll make out in this country all right. Don't let anyone tell you differently."

The four exhausted travellers climbed aboard the sleigh. The light was doused and then the teamster touched the backs of the horses lightly with the reins. They moved slowly, plodding one foot in front of the other, travelling due north, skirting the east side of two large islands. It took over half an hour, but finally, when they rounded a point of land, they sighted the low buildings of the camp dead ahead. The horses kept their steady pace until they arrived.

The teamster stood up and threw the reins in the air. "Hey you shantymen," he shouted at the top of his voice. "You lazy shantymen, get out here and help us!"

A man came to the door of the shanty, then stuck his head back inside. "Come and see who's here," he said in amazement. "It's the crazy teamster, travelling through the night!"

CHAPTER 5

THE sleigh was suddenly surrounded by forty shouting, excited shantymen who had poured out of the shanty. They were shocked to see a sleigh arrive at that isolated place two hours after sunset.

"What are you drivin' your sleigh through on a night like this, O'Riley?" one of them shouted.

The teamster was exhausted, but the sight of the other men gave him new strength and he answered bitterly. "It was MacInnes here. He forced us to come on through even when I knew better. A man like that could kill someone with his ignorance!"

The Scottish shanty clerk huffed himself up as large as he was able. "I'll have you know, I'm the shanty clerk here. Have you no respect for your superiors, O'Riley?"

"No, never again, MacInnes. Not for you, anyway. You almost killed the boy, and it's a wonder the horses didn't drop from exhaustion. We could have been stuck out on the trail all night, and it would have been your fault."

As the clerk climbed down from the sleigh he was surrounded by men, but he was still defiant. "You shantymen. You'll never learn to have respect and you'll never have the type of discipline that it takes to be good workers. I'd fire the lot of you if I had my way!"

He pushed through the crowd, keeping his superior air, and disappeared into the foreman's shanty.

O'Riley was in a fit of rage. "Damn you, MacInnes. Your time is coming!" The other men murmured their agreement under their breath. MacInnes was universally hated, but few of the shantymen had the nerve to express their hatred openly and defy the power of the company.

But now that the shanty clerk had disappeared, the men forgot him. There was much to be done, and they all pitched in to help. A group of men took charge of the sleigh, leading the horses away to be unharnessed, rubbed down, and fed. Others helped John and Meg into the shanty, where it was warm and the delicious smell of simmering beans and fresh bread pervaded the air. The two of them collapsed on the benches.

"Why look, one of them's a lad and the other's a young girl," said Tim, a young Irishman. "What brings the two of you here?"

"We're here to work," answered Meg.

"We've got a woman cook. Isn't that enough?" he said good-humouredly.

A big, strong woman was suddenly standing beside them. It was Mrs. Ferguson, the cook. "We'll have none of your comments, Tim McGuire. The woman that can't outwork you is a poor specimen." The men grinned. Mrs. Ferguson was not a person to cross words with.

"Now what is it that this teamster's done to the two of you? Such young children to be comin' into a rough shanty like this. It's a crime I tell you. O'Riley, you've got these two youngsters exhausted. What sort of a man are you?" But she did not give him a moment to explain. "Here, let's see your hands and feet."

John and Meg peeled off their mittens but neither could unlace their boots because their hands were so numb with cold.

"Cameron! Cameron! Come here!" Mrs. Ferguson ordered. "Help this boy with his boots."

A short, powerfully built man in his late thirties bent down to help John while the cook unlaced Meg's boots. He had a calm sense of self-possession that marked him off as a leader. "Frozen," he said after a moment's inspection of John's toes. "Try and close your hand into a fist, son." John's knuckles were so swollen he was unable to do it.

"Same with the girl here. Another couple of hours out on a night like this and one of them could have lost some toes from frostbite."

O'Riley, standing over the children, made an effort to explain. "I tried to tell him but MacInnes wouldn't listen. He forced me to go on." The teamster was so upset he seemed close to tears.

Cameron put his hand reassuringly on his shoulder. "We know what the company men are like, O'Riley, but it's important that we resist them."

They turned their attention back to the children. "Tim, get some coal oil from the shed. We'll have to massage their hands and feet until the circulation comes back.

Tim disappeared out of the shanty while Cameron organized a group of men to start massaging. When he returned, both John and Meg dunked their hands and feet into the liquid and teams of men gently began massaging. Gradually their fingers and toes began warming with the friction and the blood started circulating freely again.

The life of the shanty relaxed as the men turned back to their own pursuits. O'Riley had been carrying mail; someone found the bag in the back of the sleigh and distributed it among the men. Almost everyone had a letter, and they quietly gathered around the roaring fire in the centre of the room to hold up their pieces of paper and read and reread those few short lines from home. Those who were not able to read, and that made up about a quarter of the men, would have a friend slowly read the message aloud.

The men sat in small groups scattered about the fire, or crouched on the bunks that lined two of the walls of the shanty. They were strong, healthy-looking men with a ruddy, robust appearance that came from spending hours in the outdoors. They were all ages from eighteen to sixty, but most of them seemed to be in their twenties or thirties. Most of the men sported beards that they had not cut for months. The style of the shanties was for a man to let his hair grow from the time he came into the bush in September or October until he went out at spring break-up.

They were colourfully dressed. All wore blue or black woollen pants held up with wide suspenders, and high-cut moccasins made of tough leather. Many had discarded their rough mackinaw coats that were worn in the bush and sat about in long red Stanfield underwear that buttoned up to their necks and came down to their wrists. As the evening wore on, they became more relaxed. It was Saturday night; there was no work the next day, and many had heard from their families for the first time in weeks.

Meg, John and O'Riley were hungry, and the cook scraped together what was left of the Saturday meal of boiled beef, beans and bread for them to eat. Neither Meg nor John could manipulate their spoons because of their swollen hands. Mrs. Ferguson began to feed Meg, and a man named Jacques helped John.

Jacques Tremblay was a French Canadian of about forty with jet black hair and beard just beginning to turn grey. He and John quickly made friends. John had learned to speak French from his friends on the streets of Ottawa, and although Jacques' English was excellent he was the only French Canadian in the camp, and he was overjoyed to find someone to talk to in his native language for a change. The two switched back and forth from French to English so quickly that those near them could not help but wonder how they could ever make sense to each other.

In that year the men in the shanties of the Ottawa Valley were about equally divided between Scots, Irish and French Canadians, but that had not always been the case. In the 1830's and 40's many poor Irish immigrants had come into the valley, and they had battled the French Canadians in the towns and cities as well as in the shanties. The battles were so intense that some even lost their lives. Within a few years the Irish had all but driven the French out of the lumber camps. But now, in 1873, much of the bitterness and rivalry between the two groups had modified and the French were accepted on equal terms. Jacques, in fact, was a man of high prestige. He was a hewer, the most highly skilled job in the shanty, and because of his experience he was looked up to by all the men.

The bunkhouse where the men slept and ate was called the camboose shanty. Others like it could be found in any of the camps of the Ottawa Valley. It was a low building, about forty feet square, with log walls about six feet high and rising to ten feet at the peak. No nails or spikes were used in construction. The only tools needed were axes to cut the logs, and augers to bore holes at the corners for dowel pins. The space between the logs was chinked with moss and strips of bark. The roof was made out of scoops — logs hollowed into troughs. One set of scoops were laid side by side from the peak to the walls with the hollow side up. The joints between them were covered with another set of scoops set hollow side down.

The centre of the shanty was the camboose. This was a square of logs in the middle of the shanty floor that was about six feet on each side. The logs retained a foot or more of earth and sand, on which a fire roared night and day from the time the shanty was occupied in the fall to spring break-up. The fire was not only the sole heat of the shanty; it was also where the cook prepared all the meals for the men. Immediately above the fire was an open hole in the roof about twelve feet square, and above that a chimney rising some five or six feet to let the smoke escape. Posts rose to the ceiling from each corner of the square of logs, and on one of them was attached an adjustable crane that swung pots over the fire. At one end of the camboose the cook buried the heavy cast iron baking kettles. Here the pots of beans simmered away, and the fresh bread baked to a golden brown.

The camboose shanty was the ideal building for living in the bush. It could be built in two days by experienced men, out of materials that were close at hand, and the tools that were needed were ones that every shantyman could use. The shanty was cramped, and there were no tables or chairs, only benches and bunks to sit on, but it was warm, and although the fire burned constantly in the centre of the room, the updraft carried the smoke directly up the chimney, leaving the shanty airy and smokeless.

John and Meg had been in the camp for half an hour, and already they were beginning to feel relaxed. The men had made them feel accepted, the food had been good, and they were warm and comfortable, though Jacques had insisted that they put on three pairs of socks and wrap their hands in rags for protection.

As John was chatting to Tim and Jacques, the shanty became suddenly silent. There, standing in the doorway, barely visible in the light of the camboose fire, stood Hardy the foreman. His huge shoulders conveyed the impression of strength and agility the match for any two shantymen. His moustache drooped in a menacing scowl. His voice boomed out, filling the room with his anger. "All right, you men. I want that sleigh unloaded now!"

He waited impatiently, but not a man moved. He was used to having his orders obeyed at once. "You heard me," he shouted again angrily, "that sleigh can't sit there all night. I want it unloaded now!"

There was silence. This was Saturday night, the shantymen's evening off, and no one wanted to do any more work, but they were afraid of Hardy. Silence, in the end, seemed the only possible answer.

Hardy moved into the centre of the shanty. The light from the camboose fire flickering in his face giving a wildness to his appearance. He looked from man to man, his anger barely suppressed.

From the back of the room a voice suddenly mocked the foreman, "Unload it yourself!"

"Who said that?" shouted Hardy at the top of his voice. No one answered. Hardy waited, getting angrier with each passing second. He hunched over as if expecting an attack, or crouching to make one. "I asked who said that?" he shouted again at the top of his voice.

For almost a minute the shanty was silent as Hardy's eyes searched from man to man. Finally, Cameron's quiet, controlled voice broke the silence: "Do you really think the man who said that will admit it to you, Hardy?"

It took Hardy a moment to take in Cameron's words. Then he replied angrily, "Are you tellin' me what to do?"

Cameron stood ten feet away, his hands lightly touching a post on the camboose, his face an expressionless mask. "It's Saturday night, Hardy. Don't you remember? These men are tired. They've been working all week and this is their only night off. Anyway, the provisions in the sleigh aren't going to get stolen and the food can't get any more frozen. It'll wait till the morning."

Hardy was speechless, He struggled to reply, but common sense was more than he could deal with. Finally, he reacted the only way he knew how. "You think you're so smart, Cameron! You spend all your time organizing a union against me. I know what you're doing! Let me tell you I could have you locked up. Do you hear? Put in jail for so long that you'll never get out. You and a lot of others with you. You just wait and see what happens!"

Cameron's face was expressionless. "We're doing nothing, Hardy. We'll just wait for you to make the decisions." His grey eyes were unblinking, and his voice was so calm it was unnerving.

Hardy stared at Cameron for a long time, and then looked from man to man as if searching for something to say. He began backing slowly towards the door, and then suddenly in a fit of frustration he shouted. "I want that sleigh unloaded and unloaded tonight. Do you hear!" He rushed through the door and slammed it behind him.

It took some time for the shantymen to relax. They were used to Hardy's attacks, but he was the foreman and could not be ignored. After he had gone, Meg leaned over and whispered to John sitting beside her, "That Hardy could kill someone."

But John recalled what had been said when they were interviewed by Mr. Percy. "Mr. Hardy's just doing his job, Meg, He's supposed to tell the men what to do."

"What are you talking about? It's stupid trying to get the men to unload the sleigh on a night like this."

"He's the foreman. The men should listen to him."

"Listen to a man like that?"

"It's his job to tell them what to do and it's their job to do it."

"But he's crazy."

"He is not. He's just making sure the shantymen obey him, that's all."

"I don't understand why you defend him, John." Before he could answer, a group sat down next to them.

Tim was angry. "I tell you, when Hardy orders us around like that we should just take him. There's more of us than them. We could join together and run this camp."

"You mean run it for Percy?" said Mrs. Ferguson.

"No, run it for ourselves!"

"Easy, Tim," said Jacques. "If we go too fast then we'll all get blacklisted and win nothing."

That was a real threat. Blacklisting was one of the most effective weapons the company used against union agitators. If a person became known as an organizer all the companies in the Ottawa Valley would refuse to hire him and he would find it impossible to get work.

But Tim would not be pacified. "I'm tired of this waiting, waiting all the time. We should do something now or the union will never grow."

Cameron was short with him. "Have patience, Tim. If we get ourselves blacklisted then there's no more union organizing in this shanty."

"But it's more than I can stand! Hardy drives us all the time. The men get fined, and we do nothing. The log chute is unsafe, and we do nothing. Bains gets killed, and we do nothing. I say we've got to start soon or we'll do nothing all season!"

O'Riley broke into a smile. "I forgot to tell you. It slipped my mind when we were taken up with other things. This boy and girl, their last name is Bains. They're the children of Angus Bains."

"Angus' children?" said Cameron in disbelief. "It can't be."

"It is. They've come to shanty to help support their family."

The group reacted impulsively. Jacques put his hand out to both of the children and squeezed their hands. Mrs. Ferguson gave both of them a hug, but could find no words to express her joy. Tim announced it to all the men in the shanty. "These children here," he shouted, "they're John and Meg Bains. The children of Angus Bains."

Then each man in turn came up to shake their hands and repeat over and over again how badly they had felt about the death of Angus Bains. And John and Meg learned that their father had been a leader of his shanty, who in the three months before his death, had welded the men into a union that was preparing to challenge Hardy and MacInnes on every issue of the running of the camp. His death had been such a setback that the men had been unable to recover; now the appearance of Meg and John reminded the shantymen of their father, and of the hope that he had given them. The two children sensed this, and it made them feel welcome.

But they felt a new sense of nagging doubt. What did Tim mean when he said that they had done nothing when their father was killed? He was hinting at the same thing that O'Riley had talked about and their mother had suggested. They all implied that there was something strange about the death. John was trying to pose a question in his mind when everything in the shanty was drowned out by the sound of music.

One of the men had taken a fiddle from his bunk, and, after a moment to tune the strings, he began to play a lively tune. Soon a harmonica joined him and the men began to clap their hands in rhythm. The glow of the fire from the camboose reflected in the smiling happy faces of the shantymen, the corduroy floor bounced to the stamping feet, and shouts and yips mingled and became part of the music. In a moment an old shantyman was on his feet singing "The Lumber Camp Song."

When the song was over the fiddler changed his pace abruptly into a fast driving reel. Tim, the young Irishman, was on his feet dancing a jig with his arms beside his body and his feet bouncing out the rhythm of the music. Mrs. Ferguson, the cook, joined him and then half the men of the shanty were dancing to the fast rhythm of the tune. Everyone was completely involved in the music. It whirled faster and faster and the jig maintained its pressing pace until finally, with a flourish, the fiddler brought his music to a close. The men were on their feet shouting and clapping their appreciation.

Another dance was started almost immediately. The fiddle and harmonica wailed away, the men danced until the sweat soaked their long hair and red undershirts. All week they had been held to the hard discipline of their work, but this was Saturday night, their one opportunity to be completely free, and they danced with such abandon that it seemed they were drunk in spite of the fact that no man had touched liquor since they had come to shanty four months before.

John and Meg's exhaustion began to take its toll. They wanted to stay awake to watch the dancing but slowly each drifted off to sleep. Jacques and Cameron eased them into their bunk side by side, and moments later they were asleep.

Suddenly, they woke with a start. It was as if everyone was frozen in time: the music had stopped, the dancers were motionless in the centre of the room, men who had been clapping in rhythm held their hands in mid-flight, the fiddler and harmonica players still held their instruments poised as if ready to play. John peered through the dim glow of the camboose fire and there, standing in the middle of the room was Hardy flanked by MacInnes.

All eyes were fixed on Hardy, waiting expectantly for what everyone knew would happen. The big man's angry voice filled the shanty. "I want to know why that sleigh isn't unloaded!"

Hardy's huge frame stooped over as if he was readying himself for an attack. The red scar on his cheek pulsed and twitched; his fists clenched and unclenched. He waited for a long moment and then shouted again at the top of his voice. "I want all of you men out there unloading that sleigh and that's an order!"

A man sitting on a bunk not far from John spoke with a biting edge to his voice so that everyone in the shanty could hear. "Unload it yourself, Hardy!"

That was the second time that evening an anonymous voice had come to mock him, and Hardy could suppress his anger no longer. He rushed around the log frame containing the camboose in three giant strides. With one hand he grabbed the undershirt of a man sitting close by and jerked him to his feet in one pull of his bearlike arms. "Did you say that?" he shouted into the shantyman's face.

The man was terrified. "No sir! No sir! I didn't," he said, cowering to get out of the big man's way.

Hardy brushed him aside, and then saw John watching from his bunk. In a second his two arms wrenched the boy out of his bunk and held him writhing on the floor as he shook him by the shirt. His face was wild with rage, his teeth were clamped tight, his eyes had the strange, intense look of madness about them. "Did you say that, boy?" he shouted, shaking John with all his strength. "It's just the type of thing a Bains would do! You're just like your father!"

"No, no!" John shouted fearfully, twisting to get out of the way. "I didn't do it, sir! Honest I didn't!" But he was held immobile in the viselike grip of Hardy's huge hands.

"Yes you did. I know you did! You're just like your father!" Hardy's open hand was raised to strike the boy with full force.

"No, no!" John shouted, cowering back from the blow. Suddenly Meg was on Hardy's back holding onto his arm to stop him from hitting her brother. "Stop it! Stop it!" she shouted, and she pulled his hair as hard as she could and wrestled his arm.

Hardy howled in rage. He threw back his arm and sent Meg sprawling onto the bunks. He stood up, ready to hit her, but in a moment Cameron had his arm, Tim was around his neck, and others got a handhold on the big man.

Hardy was dazed and surprised at this new attack. With an enormous effort he pushed back. He was so strong that the men lost their grip and careered across the floor.

Cameron was on his feet. "Keep away from those children!" he shouted, his finger jabbing the air. "Keep away from them. You've already done enough to the Bains family!"

Hardy squared off against Cameron, "You shut up. I've had enough from you tonight!" The men stood five feet apart. Hardy towered over everyone.

Cameron was more controlled, but his eyes followed every movement of the big man. "I'll not be quiet!" He shouted in return. "Because John is the son of Angus Bains doesn't mean you should pick on him!"

"Who says I'm picking on him?"

"I do. You'll not harm him the way you harmed Bains!"

"Are you accusing me of anything?"

"You're a vicious man, Hardy. You're capable of doing anything."

Hardy was uncontrollable. In a second he dropped his head and rushed at Cameron, butting him in the chest with all his force. Cameron reeled back, falling over benches and men. He was halfway to the floor when Hardy landed on him with his full force. Cameron was down. Hardy's fist pounded him in the face. Cameron's head smashed against the floor. Hardy raised his fist again when suddenly Jacques had his arm and a group of men were on his back pulling him off Cameron.

Hardy swung out at Jacques but missed. There were shouts from the shantymen. "Let's get him!" "Kill him!" One of the younger men flashed his knife, ready to use it.

Hardy backed against the wall with MacInnes beside him. They seemed to be ready for a final attack, but Jacques kept his head. "Put that away!" he ordered the shantyman carrying the knife, and then turned back to Hardy. "Leave now before something else happens."

Hardy was unmoved. His fists were held ready for another attack, but MacInnes was pulling at his sleeve. "Hardy, come away! Come away now!" pleaded the shanty clerk.

For the first time Hardy seemed to listen to someone else. He stared at Jacques and at the others, and then, as if finally perceiving what MacInnes said, he carefully backed towards the door and the two slipped away.

A group helped Cameron to his feet. "Are you hurt?" one of the shantymen asked.

Cameron felt his chin and the back of his head. "I think it'll be all right." He seemed to shake himself. "Hardy seems to get worse every day. We'll have to watch that he doesn't try to kill us all."

CHAPTER 6

IT was Sunday, the day of rest for the shantymen, but not for Meg and John Bains, the cook's help. The men slept until eight, well past their normal rising time, but the cook roused John and Meg at six in the morning to do their chores. It was still pitch black outside when the two of them ran through the cold to the woodpile, stacked their arms with split pine and birch logs and then staggered back to the camboose shanty. They returned time and time again until they had hauled more than a cord of wood inside, and Mrs. Ferguson was satisfied that they had enough to last the day.

The morning's chores had just begun. The cook had been preparing dough for the breakfast bread and Meg was set to work kneading a large heavy mass of the sticky stuff in the big wooden bowl that was used for the purpose. When she finished, her arms and back were aching from the strenuous work. Mrs. Ferguson covered the bowl with a damp cloth and left it close to the fire to rise.

John was given the job of helping prepare the beans. First, the dried beans had to be thoroughly washed and then left to soak in water until they became soft. The cook then took a large iron pot with a tight-fitting lid and ladled in a layer of beans, then a layer of thick slices of salt pork, then a layer of beans, then more pork until the pot was filled to the brim. The seasoning of salt and blackstrap molasses was added and the pot was buried deep in the hot ashes and sand of the camboose to simmer away for hours. The longer the mixture cooked the better it became, so the cook would prepare the breakfast batch of beans the night before and the evening meal the first thing in the morning.

The other staple part of the shantyman's diet was bread. It was made an hour or so before each meal by putting the dough in tight-fitting baking kettles and burying them in the sand of the camboose. Finally, the meal was washed down with bitter-tasting black tea that was constantly simmering over the fire in a large pot suspended on a crane from a corner post of the camboose.

The meals were monotonous. On special occasions Mrs. Ferguson would dig into her larder and find apples, raisins, or nuts that she had been saving, but normally they would eat the same thing day after day, week after week, from the beginning of the season to the end.

After they had finished, the cook took Meg and John down to show them the waterhole. The ice on the lake was over a foot thick. Early in the season they had chopped a hole to get water and they always returned to the same spot. It was out of the way, a hundred feet down the shore from the camp so that one of the horses or men would not stumble into it by accident. The snow of the previous day covered everything, making the hole difficult to find, and when they did find it, it was covered by three inches of ice. John had brought along an axe and with a couple of swings the water hole was cleared. Mrs. Ferguson went back to the shanty, leaving the two children to fill the pails. With Meg's help John slowly dipped them into the waterhole.

They rested for a moment. The sun was beginning to rise in the east over a low rounded set of hills, lighting a cloudless, grey-blue sky. The dark tree-covered hills rose abruptly from the white of the snow-covered lake. It was very still: the air was motionless, the trees stood as if frozen, the place somehow seemed calm and peaceful and yet still wild and unpredictable.

They went back to their chores. John staggered back to the shanty with the yoke over his shoulder carrying the weight of the two brimming pails of water. Meg helped pour them into the large pot suspended over the camboose fire. Then John was sent to take firewood into the foreman's shanty while Meg helped spoon the dough into the large baking kettles that were buried in the sand of the fire.

Minutes later the cook roused the teamsters from their bunks. The two children were allowed to sit down until the others were dressed, and then they went out to the stable to feed the horses and oxen. Already both John and Meg were tired and the day had barely begun.

By eight, breakfast was ready and the shantymen lined up around the camboose holding their tin plates and cups. The lid of the pot containing the beans and salt pork had been removed and the delicious smell went through the whole shanty. The mixture had been simmering so long that the fat of the pork and fibres of the meat had broken down and mixed with the beans. The bread had finished baking and the men took their knives and cut off huge steaming chunks that had baked a golden brown. The tea had been simmering for over an hour and it was black and strong the way the shanty-men liked it. Everyone served themselves and then went to their bunks or sat on the benches and silently ate with their knives and homemade wooden spoons.

One of the firm rules of the shanties was that no man talked during mealtime, and Mrs. Ferguson stood beside the camboose all through the meal watching to see that the rule was followed. In the Ottawa Valley lumber camps the cooks were masters of the shanty. Not only were they in charge of preparing all the food, but they indicated where a man would sleep, stow his bags and hang his clothes to dry. Mrs. Ferguson had been coming to shanty for ten years since her husband had been killed, and she ruled her shanty with an iron hand. The man who fell out with her was bound to have a miserable season. And yet everyone knew this was just her way of maintaining order. Underneath it all she was as warm and understanding as any person could be.

After breakfast the men set out to do their Sunday chores or simply relaxed after their six days of back-breaking work. Just inside the door of the shanty there were two large hogsheads that had been split in half to make wash tubs. Some of the men hauled water from the lake, heated it over the fire and began washing their clothing with the strong potash soap that they had brought from home. Other men took needle and thread and sewed up their ripped and worn clothing. A few of the men examined their axes and sharpened them on the grindstones that were just outside the door, and others got out files and began sharpening the big crosscut saws. Five or six took axes and fishing line and headed out onto the lake to chop holes in the ice and fish for lake trout.

But the children had work to do. Right after breakfast John was sent out to the woodshed attached to the stable to split firewood, and Meg helped Mrs. Ferguson clean up around the shanty. Meg was anxious to get outside to help her brother. She did not like to be stuck inside with the cook while he was outside. As soon as she finished stacking the tin cups and dishes and sweeping around the shanty she asked to be allowed to help him. When Mrs. Ferguson agreed, she put on her heavy mackinaw and went out to find her brother.

Preparing firewood was one of the vital jobs in the camp. Early in the season a small crew of men had gone into the bush near the shanty and cut some of the dead, dry timber for the shanty fires. They hauled it back to the woodshed, cut it into two-foot lengths and stacked it to dry. Every day, in midwinter, the camboose burned close to a cord of firewood, and the foreman's shanty another half a cord. It was the job of the cook's help to split the wood, and because they had been without one for most of the season there was little left in the pile.

John went into the shed to keep out of the bitterly cold wind as he split the wood. A log was set in place and then he swung the heavy ten-pound axe in an arc over his head. It bit into the birch log without splitting. He wrestled to get it free, and then swung again. Over and over he swung the heavy axe until finally the log split. He tried another piece and again had the same problem, but he struggled on with grim determination until his shoulder blades were stiff from hefting the heavy axe and his hands were covered with red blisters.

Meg found him covered in sweat. He seemed so exhausted that she wondered if he might not collapse again. John was glad to see her. He set the axe aside and the two sat on the woodpile to rest.

"Is it hard work?" Meg asked.

John was rubbing his eyes. "I feel so tired I could curl up on the ground and sleep forever."

"Oh John, maybe we shouldn't have come. Maybe we'll get sick from being so tired all the time."

"We've got to stay, Meg. How else can mother and the children get support?"

"But you're so tired. We're both so tired."

John tried to reassure her. "We've got to try, Meg. We've got no choice now."

Soon they were talking about home. They shared stories about friends and school. They wondered aloud how their family was getting along on the small income they were earning. The more they talked the more homesick they became. It all seemed so far away, and the hardships of shanty life so close and real. After sitting a few minutes John felt a chill and the two of them went back to the camboose shanty for him to put on a sweater and warmer socks.

Inside a number of men spoke warmly to both of them. Cameron was mending John's shirt that had been ripped in the scuffle with Hardy. John made a point of thanking him. Cameron nodded and then said quietly, "A group of us will meet to talk about the union after supper. We'd like you and Meg to join us."

John felt an immediate tightening of his stomach. What would he do if they started talking about illegal activities? But he smiled and nodded agreement, hoping he had covered up his anxiety.

The cook called: "John, MacInnes was in to see me. It seems you didn't leave enough wood in the foreman's shanty this morning to keep a wolf warm. Take him some more before he complains again."

The two of them went back to the wood shed. Meg tried her hand at splitting while John gathered up an armful of wood and headed for the foreman's shanty. Inside, the building was much roomier and more comfortable than the camboose shanty. There were three beds with straw mattresses, an iron stove in one corner, a number of wooden chairs scattered around, and a large table in the middle of the room. When John entered, MacInnes was crouched over his ledgers and accounts scattered on the table. There were no windows in the shanty and he worked in the light of a coal oil lantern.

"We need a lot of wood to keep this shanty warm," he said. "In the mornings we expect you to fix the fire and fill up that box beside the stove. Do that first thing and don't forget."

"Yes, sir." John replied submissively. MacInnes struck John as a strange man. On the one hand he acted superior to the lowly cook's help, ordering him around in a haughty authoritarian manner, but on the other he seemed insecure and nervous. This was exaggerated by the peculiar impression his appearance gave. He was small and wizened, and his small hands moved nervously on the table. His eyes seemed weak as he squinted under the lamp, studying every movement of the boy as if trying to discern some weakness.

John travelled back and forth from the woodshed to the foreman's shanty five times before the box was full. Each time he came into the shanty the clerk continued to watch his movements carefully. On his last load, the shanty clerk ordered the boy to sit at the table with him. John was wary. There was something dangerous and devious about the shanty clerk, but still he was one of the bosses and had to be obeyed.

MacInnes put his hands behind his head and leaned back in his chair. A smile hung on the corners of his mouth as if he felt satisfied with a new plan of action. "How do you like being a cook's help, Bains?" he said, trying to ease into a conversation.

"It's fine, sir, thank you." MacInnes watched John carefully. "You're polite, for being from these parts."

"Yes, sir."

MacInnes paused for a long time. "Yes boy … I imagine you want to have a good season, don't you, and make lots of money for yourself and your mother? I bet you're really a good lad, underneath it all." MacInnes smiled. "I think you probably really want to help your mother." John waited warily for what would come next. "It would be a shame if you got sent back home before the season's end and you had to try to explain it."

"What do you mean, sir?" MacInnes seemed to be implying a threat.

"Just what I say. All the men in the shanty have to co-operate with the foreman and the shanty clerk. Isn't that right? And if they don't then they have to be paid off and sent back home."

"You don't have to worry about me, sir. I'll co-operate. I have to have this job to support my mother and the family." John was starting to feel frightened.

MacInnes smiled to himself. "That's a good lad. I'm glad to hear it." The light from the coal oil lantern reflected on his reddish hair and beard. His eyes narrowed and his hand stroked the stubble on his cheek. "The truth is, boy, that we need lots of co-operation this year. The men think they can start a union against us. You were there last night to see how they treated Mr. Hardy. It was a terrible thing, treating their foreman that way. Don't you think, boy?"

John looked down at his hands, remembering how Hardy had viciously attacked him. He did not want to answer the question.

MacInnes spoke sharply. "I asked if you thought what happened last night was a bad thing! What's your answer, boy?"

John nodded in agreement. The longer he stayed in the foreman's shanty the more he distrusted MacInnes' reasons for keeping him there.

MacInnes leaned back in his chair. "Mr. Hardy's a good man and works hard to help all the men as best he can. Why, if it wasn't for him and if it wasn't for the Percy Lumber Company the men wouldn't have jobs at all. They should all be grateful. That's the truth, and they should do everything to try and help Mr. Hardy rather than fighting him by starting a union. Don't you think that's true, boy?"

Again John nodded silently, looking at his hands to avoid MacInnes' gaze. Suddenly, John got to his feet.

"Thank you sir, but I must be going now. The cook'll be looking for me."

"You'll sit until I'm finished with you, boy!" Mac-Innes shouted suddenly. John sat back in his chair. Mac-Innes settled back again and tried to pick up the thread of his ideas. After a moment he brought up the union again. "I suspect that some of the men have been after you to join the union. They've probably even spoken badly of Mr. Hardy and myself. Is that right, lad?"

John said nothing. He did not want to betray his friends. He glanced at MacInnes and saw the half smile on his face as if he was getting pleasure out of seeing the young boy squirm uncomfortably. But after a moment he continued. "Let me tell you, boy; the union will not succeed. The men think they're so smart, but we know everything. We're going to fire the ringleaders. Then they can find their own way back to Ottawa, and then they can starve for the rest of the season. We're going to blacklist them. That's what we're going to do, and then they won't be able to get a job in any of the shanties through the Ottawa Valley. That'll teach them to make a union against us!"

MacInnes had become excited as he explained their plans. His eyes widened and he used his small hands to emphasize each point. Now he was quiet, carefully watching John's reaction. The boy shifted nervously.

MacInnes pushed back his chair, a superior look of victory on his face. "Yes it certainly would be nice if you could stay the season with us, lad, and I think your mother would be happy if you could bring back a full season's wages. But let me tell you, if you join with the others who are organizing the union then we will find out about it and you'll be blacklisted with the rest of them and never work in another shanty in the Ottawa Valley." He leaned over to emphasize his point. "Do you understand what I mean?"

"Yes sir. I understand sir."

John felt trapped. He wanted to be as far away from this grilling as he could get, but MacInnes was unmoved. He sat with his hands behind his head, a half-smile on his face. The light from the coal oil lantern flickered dimly in the darkened cabin, making the shanty clerk seem inscrutable and dangerous.

Suddenly MacInnes leaned forward again. "I want to be honest with you, lad," he said. "The truth is that Mr. Hardy doesn't like you or your sister Meg. He sees you as troublemakers just like your father. I tried to argue with him, saying we should give you a chance, but he won't listen. The least little bit of trouble and he's going to fire the both of you … put you on the blacklist. I don't know if I can argue against him, lad. After all, Mr. Hardy is the foreman."

John felt desparate."It's not fair, sir. I've had nothing to do with the union!"

MacInnes' face was half in shadows in the yellow light of the lantern. "I know that, lad. But Mr. Hardy's a stubborn man." He paused for a moment, a look of satisfaction on his face. "Now there may be one way. If you were to listen to what the men were saying and find out who's organizing the union, then maybe I could help you with Mr. Hardy. All you have to do is tell me about it and then we'll deal with the unionists in our own way. They don't have to know what you've done, or where we got our information. Will you do that, lad?"

John did not know how to answer. MacInnes wanted him to be an informer, and that would mean betraying the shantymen.

They were quiet for a long time, and then MacInnes prodded him again. "I want an answer, boy! Those men who are trying to organize the union want to destroy this company. They have to be stopped and dealt with harshly. I want you to help us."

MacInnes waited again for an answer. John put his head in his hands and tried to think clearly. The shanty clerk had him trapped. If he did not agree with him then he would think he was a member of the union, and he could be fired. The threats were real. What would their mother do without their wages? What work could he do if he got blacklisted? But then what would happen to the men who were organizing the union if he informed on them? And what of his father? He was somehow tied up in all of this, but he was not sure how. John was at a complete loss.

"What's your answer, boy? I want to know now!" But John could not decide. Suddenly he jumped to his feet and rushed to the door.

"Don't go!" shouted MacInnes after him. "I want an answer!"

But John was through the door and gone.

CHAPTER 7

As soon as he ran out of the foreman's shanty John was sure he had made a mistake. He felt certain that MacInnes would not let the matter drop.

Meg sensed something was wrong as soon as her brother returned to the shed. She watched him slowly walk across the dirt floor and sit on the pile of wood, deep in thought. He seemed troubled and upset: his shoulders sagged, his eyes were fixed on the floor, and his pale delicate face was lined with worry.

Meg's first impulse was to console him, but she felt he would become annoyed. Finally, she could hold back no longer. "What is it John? What's the matter?"

For a moment he seemed startled. Then he almost blurted out the details of the conversation with MacInnes. It was a burden he needed to be rid of, but he held back. He had to be certain what he was going to do. If the company was right, then it was his duty to inform on the men to MacInnes, but if they were right then he would have to join with them and try to establish the union. It was such an important question that he did not even dare to tell Meg. He had to decide by himself and make sure that he was right. But how was he to decide? That was the question. He needed time.

John smiled weakly in an effort to cover his internal conflict. Then he got to his feet and took the axe from his sister. "I'm just tired, that's all. We both need some sleep." Meg seemed satisfied with his reply.

They both got through the morning on sheer determination. John had his fear of MacInnes to contend with, and the uncertainty about the union, but by far the most pressing problem was exhaustion. As the morning wore on they took turns wielding the heavy axe. Soon their hands were covered with red, broken blisters, their backs ached and their feet were cold from the hard frozen ground. The overwhelming weariness finally was taking its toll.

By the time the lunch bell rang, John and Meg were so stiff and tired from the work and cold they found it difficult to walk. They had worked seven hours with only a brief rest for breakfast. In spite of splitting wood for over three hours the pile seemed to have scarcely grown. How would they ever be able to split the cord-and-a-half needed every day for the shanties?

But once inside the camboose shanty their spirits rose. The men joked with them about the hard work and how they had been spoiled with soft living in the city. Because of their age, the shantymen treated them more like their own children or families than as work-mates. Their warmth and affection made them feel at home.

After a light lunch Mrs. Ferguson gave the two of them the afternoon off. They climbed into their bunks and within moments they had drifted off to sleep. When Meg awoke the sun had long since set. The glowing light from the camboose fire dimly lit the room, showing the men lining up to serve themselves supper. They had tin plates and cups in their hands and waited their turn to get at the steaming pots of food on the camboose.

Meg shook her brother awake and the two of them scrambled out of their bunks.

Meg went up to the cook, fearing she would be annoyed that they had slept the whole afternoon, but the big woman smiled good-naturedly. "I had enough help today, but tomorrow will be different. The men will be back to work and you'll have to put in a full day."

John and Meg got their utensils and joined the lineup of shantymen. Already their appetites were enormous, and they served themselves heaping portions of beans, pork, bread and tea. As a special Sunday treat Mrs. Ferguson stood at the end of the line giving each person an apple. They ate in silence with the cook watching to see no one broke her rules, and it was only after the men washed their plates in the wash barrel that they began to relax. Some sat and chatted, others finished their chores and a number wrote letters home. O'Riley would be returning back down the Opeongo Line the next day and would post the mail when he got to Renfrew.

Both Meg and John wrote their own letters to their mother. Meg wrote about the trip and how glad they were to get to the Cache Lake shanty. John talked about the men in the camp, thinking it would put her at ease to know that these men had been good friends of their father. But neither of them mentioned the things that were preying on their minds. They said nothing about how MacInnes almost got them trapped in the bush, or Hardy's attack, and they did not write about the activities of the union. They did not even mention how they missed the family and their feelings of homesickness.

It was better not to have her worry about things she could not control.

The two were chatting about home when Tim McGuire came over and mentioned quietly that the meeting about the union was about to begin. Back in a corner of the shanty a small group was already talking. Jacques Tremblay was there, and Mrs. Ferguson, O'Riley, and Cameron, their leader. Along with Tim, these were the active trade unionists on the Cache Lake Limit.

This was not an open meeting. Every one of the unionists was sworn to secrecy. Union organizing had recently been legalized in Canada, but there was still some truth to the threat that police would be brought in if there was any trouble, for it was still considered sedition to encourage workers to strike against an employer.

After Meg and John joined the group, Cameron brought the meeting to order. He summarized some of the news so the discussion could be focused on the issues. "O'Riley here tells us there is trouble in the shanties throughout the Ottawa Valley. Everywhere unionists are being fired and blacklisted from the camps. What's worse, it looks grim for next year. The price of squared timber is expected to be low in Quebec this fall and that means the company will ride the men, trying to keep their profits high. But, on the other hand, O'Riley says that across the valley the shantymen are more and more anxious to establish a union. The Ottawa Trades Council, made up of all the unionists in the city, have given us their support and have even said they are willing to help us in our fight."

Cameron spoke in a clipped efficient style, giving the impression of strong inner control. "Is there anything else, O'Riley?"

The teamster smiled in his good-natured manner. "You overdraw the good rather than the bad, Cameron. It's not easy organizing a union among the shantymen. It's said that in the Gatineau shanties the companies found out who the union men were and blacklisted every one of the leaders. Conditions this winter are getting harder. The company men are no fools. They've got all the power and they'll blacklist a union man without any thought for him or his family."

The unionists were silent, thinking about the hardships and danger waiting for their friends and possibly themselves. More than one union man had given up hope because the task seemed impossible. There was not a shanty in the Ottawa Valley where the union had been able to force a company to raise wages or improve working conditions. Everywhere the unionists faced the threat of losing their jobs and their whole way of life. In spite of these great odds they persisted in their fight.

After a few moments Cameron started again. "Our situation is desperate in this shanty. Hardy is getting more and more ruthless. He's willing to use any amount of force to get his own way. Then we have MacInnes, who is the schemer, setting the plots and traps for us. It seems like it's all worked out where MacInnes is the brains and Hardy is the muscle. The fight with him last night shows how far they are willing to go just to terrify us."

"We did badly last night!" said Jacques. "Hardy wants us to fight with him because he is big and strong and can defeat us all."

Cameron nodded. "Fighting just plays his game because he can intimidate us. If we could only ignore him and wait until Percy comes up in the spring then we'd have a better chance of winning."

"But how can we ignore him?" asked Tim.

"It's hard, but we've got to do it."

"But when he starts to beat up young John here we've got to stand up and be stronger and tougher than he is."

"It's hard," said Jacques, "but maybe if we had only pulled him off of the boy and not tried to fight with him… "

"But that's backing down," said Tim, interrupting. "The men look to us, and we've got to lead them and try to stop Hardy."

"All he'll do is fire us, Tim. Don't you see?" replied Cameron with annoyance. "Then the union is finished."

Tim's impatience showed in his voice. "You want to back down all the time. You'll let Hardy make fools of us and do nothing to stop it. We've got to stand up and fight. The only way the men in the shanty are going to look up to the union is if we will make a stand against him."

"Hardy wants us to fight, Tim, then he can use that to blacklist us whenever he wants."

"I don't like it," said Tim angrily. "We've got to back down from him all the time … that's what you're saying … and I say that we can't back down or we'll never make a union. The men will be too scared."

Mrs. Ferguson interrupted. "You think it'll be easy, Tim. As if all we have to do is stand up to him and then he'll roll over and agree to everything we say. I've known him too long and I know the way Percy operates. They won't give in to a union unless they're forced into it."

"All I'm saying is that we have to stand up and fight or we'll never get anywhere. The other men will stand behind us and that's all we need. Either they give in to us or they'll never get their timber out. Hardy knows that. Remember they don't want to go broke."

O'Riley spoke. "If we show our hand too soon we'll be blacklisted, Tim. They'll fire the leaders and that'll be the end of the union. That's what they're doing in the other shanties and it'll happen here. Then you'll never get another job and a fat lot of help you'll be to the union."

Tim was unrelenting. "Don't you see that that's what Hardy's counting on. He'll terrify us to the point where we never strike … We'll be afraid to strike 'cause we think he might blacklist us. Then we do nothing. I don't know how much more I can take of that man riding us all the time. I joined the union to do something for the men, but all we do is sit and talk, talk, talk, while Hardy goes around and beats us up, and forces us to work on that unsafe log chute, and then gives us fines for nothing. I tell you I can't put up with it that much longer."

"You don't have any idea what it's like Tim," said Mrs. Ferguson. "If we rush into it they'll defeat us … you can be sure of that. It's all right for you because you're single, but there are men here with wives and children to support. They can't afford to be put on the blacklist."

Tim would not give up. "I still say that's just what Hardy's counting on. If only we could strike and show him we can stick together, even for a few days, then I'm sure we could win all of our issues."

"You'll ruin the union if that's what we do," said the cook. "You're a hothead, Tim McGuire. We've got to be sure the time is ripe."

Cameron broke into the argument, trying to bring it back to a more reasonable level. "We have to learn to fight the company, not ourselves," he said with a smile. "The rule of democracy we've all agreed on is that the majority decides what we do, and it seems that most of us agree we should wait and grow stronger before we call a strike. But our time is coming, Tim. Don't get discouraged. Someday we're going to defeat the company and we'll be the power in this shanty."

Cameron's remarks seemed to dissolve some of the tension. "Anyway," he continued, "this is the first union meeting for John and Meg and all they see is us arguing. They'll wonder what kind of union their father founded."

"No, no," Meg answered. "It's good to see the union is important."

"We'd like you to join," said Cameron. "Because of your father, we think it will be important to the others if you take an active part."

"Yes, we'd like to. Isn't that right, John?" Her brother sat without a hint of emotion on his face. "Anyway, what did father do in the union?"

Cameron smiled. "Everyone looked up to your father in this shanty. And because he was in favour of the union, and fought for it, the others followed him. That's why his death was such a blow to us all."

Tim interrupted insistently. "And it wasn't an accident. That's the thing!"

"You can't say that, Tim. You know we've got no proof that he was murdered." They had argued the question endlessly, and it annoyed Cameron that it was being brought up again.

"There's just too many funny things about his accident. There was the fact that he was all alone at the time it happened, and the fact that it was only his head that was damaged. It's just too strange that a shantyman as experienced as Angus would be killed by a falling tree."

"But we have no proof, Tim! If there was proof then we'd all want to do something. But we have nothing!"

"That's all you ever say, Cameron," said Tim in frustration. "We're the union and Bains was our leader. We should do something about it, but we do nothing! nothing!"

Cameron's voice cracked with rage. "We can't do anything, Tim … you know that! We've been over and over this, again and again, and we always come to the same conclusion. So why do you keep bringing it up?"

"We're the union. We owe it to Bains. That's all!"

Finally, Cameron shrugged his shoulders in resignation. "Tim, I don't know what more we can do. If we could show that Bains was murdered then none of us would rest until the person who did it was punished. But we can't prove it."

Jacques interrupted the argument. "Since Bains was killed we seem to argue too much. It is important that we find agreement or we can never make the union. Let's try and be friends together."

They were quiet for a few moments, and then Meg began again in her enthusiastic manner. "I'd like to help the union. Hardy and MacInnes never think of anyone but themselves and the company."

"That's right."

"I'll do anything to be against the two of them, and what with father being so important to the union I guess it's really important that we take part. We'd like to. Isn't that right, John?"

But John was still far from convinced. He had made promises to Percy and MacInnes that he would not get involved, and the family was depending on their income. But on the other hand their father must have had a good reason for starting the union. John pushed his hands through his light sandy hair and frowned. "I don't know, I just don't know."

"What do you mean?" said Cameron in amazement.

John felt small and frail in the face of these strong shantymen, and he was almost at the point of tears, but he stuck to his beliefs. "I'm just not sure, sir."

"But why?"

"It's just that the union activity is illegal … and … and we've got to support our family, and Mr. Percy and MacInnes said they'd blacklist me, and … " his voice trailed away.

"But father was for the union, John." Meg was shocked.

"I know but … "

"We've got to support it!"

"It's Mr. Percy, Meg, and Mr. Hardy, and Mr. Mac-Innes. They'll get us, Meg. Then we'll have no job. Don't you understand?"

"You're a coward!" shouted Tim. "You're afraid of Hardy and MacInnes. Admit it!"

"No, no! It's not that!"

Tim was insistent. "You've got to choose, boy. It's between us and them."

John was desperate. Why couldn't they leave him alone? Why did he have to take sides? Why couldn't he just be the cook's help and nothing else? He buried his face in his hands.

"What good are you, boy? You won't even stand up for what your father believed in … for what he died for!"

"That's enough, Tim!" interrupted Cameron. "Leave the boy be."

"Why?" said Tim angrily. "He's the son of Angus Bains. He's got to join us!"

"I said leave him be. Everyone makes up their own mind in this union. He's only a boy. Maybe in time he'll learn what we're all trying to do. Let's leave it now. I see the other men are getting ready for bed. We'll talk again about the union and maybe next time, John, you'll understand more about the issues and want to join us."

The meeting broke up. As John was about to go, Tim suddenly grabbed his arm, squeezing it in his strong hand. "Don't you be telling Hardy or MacInnes about this meeting, John, Do you understand?"

CHAPTER 8

THERE was bitter discontent among the shantymen working on the Cache Lake Limit. In addition to Hardy's bullying and MacInnes' spying, the men were driven constantly to work harder and harder. By far the biggest cause of discontent, though, was the construction of the log chute.

The river emptying Cache Lake was the Madawaska, and although it was only a small stream this close to its source, it roared over a granite ridge dropping about fifty feet in a waterfall as it drained out of the lake. From there it tumbled another hundred yards, dropping another forty feet in total, until finally it became a placid slow-moving stream that wound its way to Lake of Two Rivers ten miles downstream.

In order to get the huge square timbers down to the market at Quebec City, they had to be floated the whole 180 miles of the Madawaska down to where it emptied into the Ottawa. There the timbers would be built into rafts for the rest of the trip. If they were to float the logs downstream they had to get them around the waterfall and rapids or they would smash to pieces on the rocks. The method that had been perfected in the Ottawa Valley was to build log chutes that would slide each log, one by one, around the fast water.

But building the chute was not easy. The men had to construct a trestle made out of logs to carry the weight of the narrow spillway of water. During the spring flood, water would be released into the spillway to carry the logs one at a time as it rushed from the lake to the river below. The shantymen had begun building the chute that winter, and it would occupy fifteen men for the whole season in order to be ready by spring break-up.

The problem was that many of the men thought the log chute was unsafe. In order to get around the waterfall, the trestle had to be built fifty or sixty feet above the ground for almost a hundred yards. This was a real engineering feat, calling for specialized skills that neither Hardy nor MacInnes had. Rather than building the trestle gradually from the bottom up, in such a way that it held together as one unit, Hardy had chosen a faster way, building it out from the top of the hill and lowering the log supports from the existing trestle. As a result, one section was standing fifty feet or more in the air, with little support, and in a wind it swayed dangerously.

Cameron worked on the chute as a rigger, and Tim worked as a teamster hauling the logs out of the bush. One afternoon John overheard several of the men discussing how dangerous the chute was, and finally Cameron was persuaded to challenge Hardy on the issue. He argued that the trestle should be built from the ground up so that it hung together as one strong, well-knit unit. Hardy would hear none of it. "Mind your own business," he said curtly. "I'm the foreman here and you'll build the trestle the way I want and no back-talk."

Cameron tried to argue, but saw that Hardy was not going to yield on the issue. For the moment, the matter was dropped.

The morale of the men sunk to a new low. Many of them tried to get assigned to other work, but when that was impossible they began working with extra caution. The work slowed, and Hardy, seeing this, would rage at the men to make them work faster. As the season wore on, he spent more and more of his time at the chute, knowing that if it were not finished by spring break-up they would never get the timber out that year. He took to peering over their shoulders, but the men only became more edgy and bad-tempered.

The morale of the men working on other jobs in the shanty was little better. Often Hardy would send Mac-Innes out to spy on them, and the sly shanty clerk would sneak through the bush trying his best to catch a man talking or resting when he should have been working. Often the men would get angry and order the clerk to leave, but it did little good. MacInnes would go directly back to Hardy, who would then levy a dollar fine against the man's wages, and anyone who protested would be fined another dollar. The company's word was law, and the shantymen either buckled under or were punished.

Because of John and Meg's inexperience, they took longer doing jobs than others, and often they were rewarded for their efforts by the bitter words of one or the other of the company men. As the first week went on, the work seemed to be getting harder rather than easier, and it was all both of them could do to survive from one day to the next. Their daily routine started at five in the morning, when the cook roused them out of their bunks.

In the next few hours, John had to haul enough firewood into the camboose and foreman's shanties for the whole day, fetch the water from the waterhole in the ice, help the teamsters prepare the animals for the day's work and then begin the back-breaking job of splitting firewood.

Meg worked inside the camboose shanty, helping the cook. She kneaded the dough, helped prepare the beans and pork and tended the camboose fire, and as soon as breakfast was over they began work on lunch. She resented being stuck in the camboose shanty while John was allowed outside, but kept quiet about it for now.

By mid-morning they had finished most of the camp chores, and John and often Meg were sent out to the men working in the bush to give whatever help they needed. The rest of the day was spent preparing lunch, fetching tools, running messages, or doing any number of chores for the men. By supper they both were exhausted, and more chores awaited them when the evening meal was finished. But they pushed on, determined to show everyone that in spite of their city upbringing they could work as hard as anyone in the camp.

The work on the Percy Limit was scattered over a wide area around Cache Lake, and that meant even more work for John and Meg. A crew of about fifteen men worked on the log chute. Another group of fifteen men worked in a rich stand of pine at the extreme north end of the lake. This was a beautiful stand of white pine, the most valuable timber of all the wood cut in the Ottawa Valley. In sandy soil the trees grew to almost six feet in diameter and close to two hundred feet high; the first hundred feet was straight and clear, with no limbs or blemishes on the wood. There were a number of crews working in the grove: fellers, sawers, hewers and teamsters, all doing their special jobs.

First, the "feller" dropped the tree in exactly the right spot, so that it did not get hung up on the trees surrounding it and was easy to work on. Once it was on the ground and cut into twenty-five to thirty-foot lengths, the "scorer" peeled the bark and scored a line along the length of the log, which marked the thickness that was to be trimmed off. The "hewers" stood on top of the log with heavy twelve-pound broad axes and trimmed the log down to the scored mark, making it as smooth as a planed board. When they had finished on one side, the log was rolled over ninety degrees and the hewer trimmed another side, and then another, until the log was a perfect square, and the same thickness all the way along. This was squared timber, cut for the British markets, that was the backbone of the Ottawa Valley lumber trade.

There were two other crews that Meg and John often had to see. One gang worked two miles northwest of the lake in a stand of red pine that extended over several acres. The other worked west of the lake, cutting a large stand of red pine that stretched along a series of ridges and ravines. The work was much more difficult here, because the shantymen had to haul the timber over tortuous roads down to the lakeside. The usual method was to wrestle the squared logs with heavy poles onto the front bunk of sleighs. Then a team of horses or a pair of oxen would drag the load over the steep twisting trails leading down to the water's edge, where it was stacked waiting for the spring breakup.

In spite of the heavy work, there were some consolations. The loneliness of the country had a strange fascination. Often they would be engrossed in their work and then glance up to find they were surrounded by the wilderness: the snow on the lake was so white it hurt their eyes, and the land was dark and rugged with streams etched into the ground by centuries of erosion. Occasionally, they saw a deer or a fox lurking at the edge of the lake. An Arctic owl had taken up residence for the winter, and often Meg or John would catch sight of the big white bird as it circled slowly in the sky, watching hungrily for prey. Rarer still, but getting ever more daring as hunger pushed them closer to the camp, were the wolves.

One dull, overcast morning about a week after they had arrived in camp, John ran a message from Hardy telling MacInnes, who was with the men working in the stand of white pine, that he wanted to see him at the log chute. Meg had arrived a short time before with the lunches for the shantymen, and after MacInnes had gone, John helped her prepare the meal. They chatted while they got the fire going, and then the boy took the yoke of pails to fetch water.

The hole through the ice was frozen an inch thick; John broke it free and scooped one pailful and then another. The wooden yoke took some of the weight around his neck as he began to struggle back up the slope towards the fire. Carefully, he picked his way over the rocks, logs and fresh-cut branches, watching the brimming pails to see they did not spill. The weight of the pails strained against his shoulders, and he felt exhaustion through his whole body. As he swung his leg over a fallen tree, carefully balancing the yoke, his foot suddenly slipped and he fell. The water spilled over his pants and boots, soaking him to the skin.

He struggled back to the fire with what remained of the water and then settled beside the fire, annoyed with himself. Every time he was busy it seemed something happened to delay him. The water in his pants had turned to crusty ice granules, and he would have to dry his clothes thoroughly or run the risk of frostbite.

He was sitting by the fire, chatting with Meg, when suddenly MacInnes appeared out of the bush.

"Aha! I caught you sitting down, boy. You're taking it easy. Now get up and start working, before I report you to Hardy!"

John jumped to his feet, his wet shoe falling out of his hands. "But sir! I was drying myself, sir! I spilled water on myself!"

"Don't give me any of your lame excuses. I caught you sitting down 'cause you thought that I'd gone. If I catch you again you'll be packing your bags. Do you understand, boy?"

"Yes sir. I understand sir, but really I was … "

"None of your excuses. Do you hear?"

"Yes sir," said John obediently.

MacInnes' mood changed into false friendliness. A smile lurked on the edges of his mouth, as if he was pleased with some plan. "What about that information you were to get for me? Where is it? I might go easier on you if I thought you might cooperate."

John fidgeted nervously and glanced at Meg, hoping she didn't understand. He was tormented. Why couldn't he be left alone?

"Give me that information about the union, Bains, and I'll go easier on you." The smile still lurked on the shanty clerk's face. Then, as suddenly as he had appeared, he walked away in the direction of the log chute.

Meg and John stood watching the spot where Mac-Innes had disappeared until they were certain he had gone for good. Then they began to relax again.

Meg sighed. "He's a terrible man. He sneaks around like he thinks we're always going to be taking time off." She settled beside the fire. "You'd better dry your leg before it freezes."

John propped his leg close to the fire. In spite of what the company man said, it would be foolish to risk frostbite.

Meg worked silently at preparing lunch for a few minutes, then looked carefully at John. "What was that about providing MacInnes with information?"

In the week they had been in the camp they had argued almost every day about the union. Meg insisted that they should support it in every way they could, but John was still undecided. Now he wanted to avoid her question, rather than bring it up again. "It was nothing," he said casually.

"But he seemed to mean that you had some information about the union."

"It was nothing, really, Meg."

"Then what did he mean?"

"Let's not argue again, Meg. The union's not important to us. Let the others worry about it. Let's just do our jobs and then go home after the season's over. That's the only safe way."

"It is important, John," she insisted. "Daddy thought it was important and so do I. I don't understand you any more."

They glared at each other in silence. This was the first big argument they had ever had, and it was creating a barrier between them. Finally, when the water boiled for tea, they called the shantymen. At least that way they could avoid the argument.

Lunch was eaten in silence. After they finished, the shantymen relaxed for a few minutes while they smoked their pipes and chatted. Soon they were talking about conditions of their work, and Jacques brought up the union, but they were interrupted by the sudden appearance of MacInnes.

"Bains," he said addressing John. "I was talking to Hardy at the log chute. He wants you to go back to the shanty and get the spare team of horses out of the stable. Harness them up and take them to him."

"Yes sir."

"Then snap to it, lad. You know Hardy doesn't like to be kept waiting."

John got on his snowshoes and was about to leave when Meg said. "I'd better come with you. Those horses are hard to handle."

John agreed and the two set off. It was close to a mile and a half back to the shanty. When they got there they immediately set about harnessing the horses. Although they had often helped others, neither of them had done it by themselves before. Sensing their inexperience, the horses shied away, tossing their heads when John or Meg tried to buckle up the heavy leather straps. But finally they were finished and led the team out of the stable by their halters. Once outside, John arranged the reins carefully in his hands and they set off.

It was not easy going. Out on the ice of the lake the wind was cold, swirling snow into their faces. The horses strained at their bits, trying to break into a run, but John held them firmly in check the way he had seen the teamsters work in the past. Slowly they made their way across the ice to the end of a large bay. There they rested for a moment, and then took a short-cut over a ridge and back out onto the lake on the other side. Finally, they guided the animals carefully around the soft ice near the outlet of the lake, and negotiated the last hundred yards along a narrow trail. When they came over the crest of the hill, Meg and John could see the crews of men working on the log chute.

It was a chaotic scene. Seven or eight men were up in the skeleton of the trestle climbing on the log supports, shouting instructions to one another. High up on the lake side of the chute, a team of horses lowered struts down the completed part of the chute until the men on the trestle were able to grasp onto them with pike poles and wrestle them into place. There were crews of men cutting supports and snaking them out of the bush, while others trimmed and cut them to exact length. Hardy was in the middle of it all, standing with his hands on his hips, shouting orders to one man or another.

When they caught Hardy's attention, the big man let out an angry shout. "Where have you been? We've been waiting for them horses for over an hour!"

Both Meg and John were frightened with the intensity of Hardy's attack. John tried to explain. "We had to harness the team, sir. Then we had to bring them all the way here. And … and they're a hard team to handle, sir."

"You didn't need all that time! Did you go in and see the cook to get something to eat? Did you have a rest?"

"No sir! We didn't really, sir!"

Hardy stood large and scowling. Other men surrounded them, waiting for the impending explosion. "Look, I'm not happy with the two of you! Not happy at all! First I hear from MacInnes that he caught you sitting down today, boy, and then it takes almost half a day for the two of you to bring a team of horses. If this doesn't improve then I'm sending you back to Ottawa. For now I'll fine each of you fifty cents, a dollar in total. Maybe that'll teach you to work harder."

John was stunned. "But … but sir. That's more than a day's pay."

"That's right, boy. Maybe you'll learn to work harder the next time and not be hanging around!"

Meg was incensed at this treatment. "You can't do that!"

Hardy turned on her angrily. "You just see if I can't, and you just watch yourself, little miss, or you'll be in more trouble than you bargained for."

Meg was going to say something more, but John pulled her arm and whispered. "Leave it alone."

"A dollar fine!" Hardy shouted. "It'll be taken out of your pay! Now get those horses over there with the others and be smart about it. And you men, get back to work. You've seen enough."

John felt such an overwhelming sense of shame and humiliation that he was close to tears, but what could they do except take the fine and hope that Hardy would leave them alone? He struggled to keep the horses in check, for now he had to walk the team down the hill and back the animals into a set of traces that were waiting. They moved skittishly, sensing that he had lost control. Suddenly Tim was there, and he took the reins out of the boy's hands.

"Easy now … easy!" he said, talking to the animals, trying to calm them. Gradually the big horses responded, and Tim was able to take them down the hill and back them into the traces. When they were shackled into place the teamster turned. "Hardy shouldn't have you working a team like that. It takes time to learn to work horses."

Meg nodded angrily. "It's not fair, Tim! We work as hard as we can but he wouldn't even let us explain!"

"I know what he's like, Meg. But the two of you will have to learn to stand up to him. If you don't he'll ride you all the time. You'll get so many fines that you won't have any wages left. Why don't you go back up there and tell him that you won't take it."

"All right, I will. Come on, John!"

"We can't do that. He'll just fine us again."

Tim's face darkened. "What is it, boy? You've got to stand up for yourself."

"I don't know … I … "

It was the indecision that Tim saw all around him that he could no longer stand. "If you won't do it then we'll have to do it for you! Come on, Meg!" Tim suddenly strode angrily up the hill towards Hardy. Meg followed and John came a few paces behind. The foreman turned to meet them. His huge, powerful figure towered over the young Irishman, his hands rested on his hips, he swayed back and forth on the balls of his feet, the jagged scar on his cheek taking on an angry purple look as he became more excited.

Tim's fiery temper made him fearless. "Hardy! Those kids are not going to put up with this fine of yours!"

"And why not?"

"Because they don't deserve a fine. They're doing as much work as they're able!"

Hardy reacted swiftly. "I'm the foreman here, and I'm not going to have people like you tell me what to do!"

"It's not fair!" Meg shouted. "We brought that team as quickly as we could."

"Listen the three of you, and listen good." Hardy's anger was barely under control. "I don't have to give a reason when I give out a fine. You either stay out of my way or you're going to be walking back to Ottawa. Do you understand?"

Suddenly Cameron was there. He had been working high up on the trestle and when he saw the argument begin he scrambled down to make sure things did not get out of control. "What's going on here?" he asked as he came up to the others.

"It's Hardy," said Tim. "He gave a fine to the two Bains and they didn't do anything to deserve it."

"It's none of your business who I fine," shouted Hardy. "And you stay out of it too, Cameron. Nobody tells me what to do in my shanty!"

"Then it's about time you didn't have that kind of power," said Cameron cooly. "These fines have gone far enough!"

Hardy went into a rage, shouting at the top of his voice, his arms flailing. "Get out of here, Cameron! I know what you want, you and your union. Well you won't get it while I'm around. I run this shanty, understand, and I always will, and you and your union are nothing! Get that straight!"

"You can't run a shanty like this. You're not fit to do it!"

"I'm the foreman here and I do what I want!" Suddenly Hardy lunged for Cameron, grabbing him by the shoulders with his hands. Cameron staggered back from the weight of the big man's body, and in seconds Hardy had an arm lock around his neck and twisted him to the ground. Cameron struggled vainly, but Hardy forced him deeper and deeper into the snow.

John was in a panic. The men were fighting over something he had started. He had to stop them before someone was hurt. He rushed forward shouting. "Stop! Stop! Please stop! I'll take the fine! I'll take the fine, Mr. Hardy! Just stop fighting, please!"

Hardy eased his grip and the two men broke apart. Both seemed to be puzzled, trying to understand what John was saying.

"I'll take the fine, sir, any fine, but don't fight like this, please!" John pleaded.

The moment of shocked disbelief changed as Hardy smiled and then burst into loud laughter. "There you are, Cameron. There's your union man. That's it, boy. You take the fine. That's the only thing to do." Then he laughed again. Hardy was on his feet and started to walk up the hill away from the men. Every now and then they could hear him break into a loud scornful laugh and then, finally, he disappeared over the crest of the hill.

All the men were quiet, waiting for John to give some explanation. He looked from man to man, not knowing what to say. Finally, Cameron asked the question that was on all of their minds. "Why did you back down, boy?"

John tried to answer. "I ... I ... had to stop the fight. Someone could have been hurt." He looked from face to face, but the men stared back.

Tim shouted in anger. "You backed down from him! You're not one of us now!" He spat in the snow disgustedly and went back to his team of horses.

Gradually the other men went back to their work, discouraged that they had lost once again, and John was alone with Cameron and Meg. The union leader studied the boy for the longest time before speaking. "You've left us, boy," he said softly. "You've left us and now you'll have to find your own way." Cameron turned and began climbing the trestle, leaving John and his sister standing in the snow by themselves.

CHAPTER 9

BY that evening a new mood of depression had settled on the shantymen, the normal joking giving way to tension and distrust. After supper they talked quietly and intently about the day's events, often looking up to stare at John with serious frowning faces as if they had been talking about him, but no one said a word to him. They were dealing with him the only way they knew how, by refusing to acknowledge that he existed.

Even Meg found it difficult to justify John's actions. More than once she started to ask her brother to explain himself, but each time she stopped. What could he say that would change things? He had chosen the side of the company, and that was the end of it.

By the time John climbed into his bunk, he felt lonelier than at any time in his life. He longed to be back at home in the security of his own family, where he would be accepted without question. He put his hands to his eyes and found his face was wet with tears; a sob caught in his throat, and he bit his lip to hold it back. Meg mustn't know he was crying. And yet what could he do? For the first time he realized what it was like to be without friends and completely alone. Finally, he overcame the sobs, and exhaustion forced him into sleep.

The next morning things were little better. The shantymen simply ignored him. Mrs. Ferguson gave him his orders with the least possible explanation. When he helped the teamsters harness the animals, no one said as much as a word to him. When he went to the shed to split wood after breakfast, he hoped desperately that Meg would seek him out so that he could explain things to her, but she avoided him as well.

The only person who talked to him was Hardy. In midmorning John happened to meet him with a group of men in the white pine grove. The foreman laughed mockingly. "There's my man," he said. "Do anything I ask. A regular company man." And then he laughed again. The others stirred restlessly but said nothing.

Overnight there had been a change in the weather. The temperature had risen close to the freezing point: in this country that usually meant a storm was on the way. Dark, heavy clouds moved quickly overhead, and by mid-morning a wind had sprung up, bending the trees back and forth. Soon it was beginning to snow big wet snowflakes that stuck to the trees and to the clothing of the men.

By noon Meg had arrived with the lunches, and the two set a fire and readied the meal without as much as a word to each other. John put on snowshoes, picked up the yoke of pails and went to fetch water. When he broke through the bush onto the lake he was surprised to see how the weather had closed in. The wind whipping across the open ice blew the snow in sheets into his face and he had to crouch to keep it out of his eyes. The trees snapped back and forth furiously, and the black clouds seemed ever more menacing. For an instant John thought of the men working high up on the unprotected log chute, and then he concentrated on what he was doing.

He had to search for a couple of minutes to find the waterhole because it was covered with snow, but when he found it he deftly chopped it free of ice with a couple of blows of his axe. He was dipping the pails when something caught his eye. There, not twenty-five yards away, crouched among some trees, was a large grey timber wolf peering out at him. It was well over a hundred pounds, with powerful neck and shoulder muscles that could force most animals to the ground and tear them to pieces in a moment.

John controlled himself. Gradually he eased the pails onto the ground, and, gripping the axe in his two hands, he crouched, waiting for the attack. The two stared at each other unblinking, as if each was daring the other to make a move, and then, without warning, the wolf turned and disappeared into the bush as if it had been a grey ghost. John went over to the spot where it had stood and peered through the trees, but there was nothing except pawprints that were fast disappearing under the new-fallen snow.

When he got back to the fire, John and Meg silently finished preparing lunch and then called the men. John sat alone, eating his lunch and drinking the strong tea. He felt completely isolated from the others, including his sister. He tried to reassure himself that his behaviour had been proper. It was wrong to fight, he thought. It was wrong to stand up to a boss. A worker has to follow orders; that was the only way a company could function. And it was wrong to start a union, because that was a threat to the company. John felt better telling himself this. Yes, he was convinced; it was wrong to stand up to those who have authority. Why couldn't the others see it like this?

The snow drove in through the trees to where the men sat. It stuck to their mackinaws and melted, making them wet and uncomfortable. Black snow clouds were sweeping across the sky. The wind whipped the trees back and forth in a violent motion, and the snow was falling harder than ever. The men pulled up their collars and huddled closer to the fire to keep warm.

Suddenly, one of the men stood up, an alert look on his face. "What was that?"

Everyone stopped and listened. "It's the wind," said Jacques.

They went back to smoking their pipes and talking in low voices. Meg heaped another log on the fire.

Next another man was on his feet. "Yes! Yes! Listen to that! It's the emergency bell!"

All the men rose at once, straining to hear. It was clear now. It was the emergency bell being rung down by the log chute!

In the sudden panic Jacques took firm control. "Grab your axes!" he shouted excitedly. "Everyone bring their own tools! John, bring the coils of rope! Meg, put out the fire! You teamsters bring the horses!" The men were running frantically in every direction to gather their equipment.

They could hear the emergency bell clearer now. It was ringing over and over again in a frantic piercing rhythm. The bell was a large iron triangle that was rung by a man holding an iron bar, clanging it around and around, louder and louder, until it could be heard for miles. It was a sound everyone in the shanties feared, because it meant some disaster had struck and every available person was needed to help.

They ran frantically down the hill towards the lake. John was carrying two coils of rope and Meg clutched a big doubleheaded axe. All around them the shantymen ran towards the sound of the bell, and behind them the teamsters could be heard shouting at their horses. Because of their snowshoes they had to go slowly down the hill, but once out on the frozen lake they ran as fast as they could, urged on by the sound of the bell and the fear of what had happened. Louder and louder it became, until it rose to an ear-splitting frenzy. John and Meg were with the first group of men, pushing themselves harder and harder, barely watching where they were going. Finally, they made it to the shore and were among the first to greet the bell-ringer. The bell stopped, and the silence was deafening.

"What happened?" someone shouted.

"It's the log chute! It collapsed in the wind! There's men trapped underneath!"

"My God!"

They ran down the hill. The whole chute had collapsed, and there was nothing left of it but a jumble of struts and braces piled haphazardly in a huge heap. For a moment they stood at the crest of the hill staring in horror at the disaster, but then they heard the moaning of injured men and they sprang into action.

They scrambled down the hill to help the others who were pulling away at logs, trying to free those trapped below. Cameron was there, hobbling on one injured leg.

Hardy worked by himself, as if scorned by the others. He seemed dazed, suffering from shock, wandering around as if looking vaguely for something to do.

The action whirled about them as the men took command with a driving sense of urgency. Meg rushed to where three men were struggling to free a log. She joined in, and then others came, and gradually they pulled the massive timber out of the tangle with their own brute strength. There was a shantyman trapped below. Someone scrambled down into the hole that had been created and pushed other logs aside, but still they could not free him. The injured man did not seem to be pinned by logs any longer, but he did not have the strength to get himself out. Meg pushed forward and wedged herself into the hole. The man's face was pale, blood crusted his lips, and he held his ribs, moaning and squirming in pain. Meg hooked her hands in his arm-pits and pulled with all her strength. Gradually she lifted the man up through the hole until the others could grab him and lift him free.

Cameron crouched over him. "Where does it hurt?" he demanded. The shantyman was doubled up in pain, holding his side. Cameron touched him gently on the chest. "Looks like he has some broken ribs. Take him to the campfire. You go with them, John, and see that he's all right."

Two of the men carried the injured man to the fire, and the others carried on with the frantic search. By the time John had a fire started there were two other injured men, and he arranged them close together so they could share body warmth. Then he went to the tool cache, found a large piece of canvas and staked it out to give the injured men shelter from the wind and blowing snow. As he was finishing, another injured man was brought in. He tended to the new arrival, built up the fire, and then went back to the scene of the disaster.

The teamsters had arrived with the horses, and they were being used to pull the logs off in an effort to free trapped men. They worked frantically, but still the work proceeded slowly because they did not want to hurt the men trapped below. After a time they had five men free, and then six. All of them were alive.

They were beginning to relax when someone shouted. "There's a man in here. He's alive!" They converged on the spot. Horses were hitched to pull away the loose logs. The ones that were too close to the man had to be lifted away by hand, but finally, after what seemed to be an eternity, the man was brought out alive.

Again they thought the rescue work was finished, until someone asked, "Where's Tim? He's still missing. He was working under the chute when it gave away."

There was a frantic search among the men, but he was nowhere to be found. The word was shouted to everyone. "Tim's missing! We have to find him!"

They began to search all over again. It had been over an hour since the chute had collapsed, and the snow had continued to swirl around them, covering everything. It was difficult to see between the logs, but on and on they searched desperately. Ten minutes passed, twenty minutes, half an hour, but no one was ready to give up. Suddenly, someone shouted frantically. "It's a hand! It's a hand! Over here!"

Everyone converged on the spot. There, away down in an opening in the logs, fingers seemed to reach skyward as if trying to grasp for help.

Four teams of horses converged on the spot. The men pushed and clawed at the logs, trying to get them out of the way. There were so many of them that they got in each other's way, but finally after backbreaking work they could see the hand, and then there was an arm, and then there was one more log to be lifted off, and they found Tim with his head crushed.

A hush came over the men. Cameron lifted up Tim's broken body in his arms and made his way down the hill to where Hardy was standing. His body shook with emotion, tears streaming down his face, "See what you've done!" he shouted desperately. "See what you've done!"

Cameron sobbed and collapsed to his knees. The body slipped out of his arms.

John and Meg and Jacques tried to console him, but they were in tears themselves. "We'll get them, Cameron!" John said. "We'll get them, and this time we'll do it for Tim and my father and all the others!"

1. The work of the lumber camps or "shanties" began in the fall before freeze-up, when the shantymen travelled by road and trail out from the cities and towns and beyond the farms where land had been cleared into the forests. After snowfall, heavy sleighs laden with provisions were driven out to the camps.

2. On the roads leading to the camps, "stopping places" like this one were spaced at the distance of a day's travel. Here the teamsters could bed down their horses, get something to eat, and find rough shelter for the night.

3. The camboose shanty, used in the Upper Ottawa River Valley in the 1870s and 80s and made out of materials found close at hand, and built with tools any shantyman could use.

4. The shanty was a log building about forty feet square. The roof was made of scooped logs placed alternately one up and one down. In the centre of the roof was a chimney made of rough planks that rose three or four feet.

5. This picture, showing a crew of shantymen, is a good illustration of the men who laboured in the camps. All ages and varieties of men came into the bush from the young "cook's help", seen on the left, to experienced hands in their fifties and sixties.

6. Inside the shanty, in the centre of the floor, was the camboose, a sand mound about six feet square, where the fire blazed from the beginning of the season to the end. The heat of the fire created a draft that sucked the smoke up the chimney. Even in the worst conditions the camboose shanty was a warm, dry haven from the harsh conditions of the bush.

7. Along the walls of the shanty were tiers of bunks where the men slept and kept their shanty possessions. Heavy woollen clothing hung everywhere as the men tried to keep their gear dry.

8. Work in the bush included a number of specialized jobs. "Fellers" took down the trees, the "liners" and "hewers" trimmed them, and the horses, driven by the teamsters, dragged the big timbers to the water's edge.

9. Only the best red and white pine were selected for the "squared timber" trade. A good feller could drop a tree in any spot he was asked.

10. Once one of the mammoth trees was on the ground, it would be carefully measured and a line would be snapped, indicating how much the hewers were to trim. The final product was a squared log between thirty and fifty feet in length.

11. This process wasted great amounts of good timber. Not only was the top of the tree discarded, but the wood on the outside of the tree, which is clearest of knots, was left to rot in the bush.

12. The men laboured in the bush six days a week from sun-up to sun-down under the most difficult conditions. By spring the horses were so lean from hard work their ribs could be counted, and the men longed for the season to be over.

13. When spring break-up came, the timber had to be driven down the rivers to market. To bypass rapids, log chutes like these were built.

14. On the drive the logs were released into the chutes one at a time, and they were flushed down to the quiet water below the rapids.

15. In spite of the use of chutes, logs still got caught on outcroppings in the river. Other logs sweeping along behind often got trapped and within moments a log jam had been created.

16. To break a jam was the most dangerous job on the drive and many a shantyman lost his life in the attempt.

17. Once the logs had been driven down the tributaries of the Upper Ottawa they were built into rafts to be taken downriver to market. This picture shows the crew eating a meal while they drifted with the current.

18. The rafts were an enormous floating carpet of logs where the men lived and worked for the six to eight weeks that it took to drift down to Quebec City.

19. At rapids or waterfalls these rafts would be broken into smaller units called cribs. The men would then take each crib, one by one, down timber slides that had been built to bypass the fast water. Once below, the cribs would be put back together into a raft and they would continue downstream.

20. On reaching Quebec City the timber rafts were broken up and the logs loaded aboard sailing ships bound for Britain.

CHAPTER 10

THE accident changed John dramatically. When they finally got back to the shanty he tried to explain it to Meg, but his words came haltingly. "I … I thought the union was wrong, Meg. It was against the company and they're supposed to be the ones to lead us. But … but they won't listen. Hardy just wants to push us all the time. And MacInnes spies on the union. They're not interested in us … in any of the shantymen in this camp. They don't even care if any of us are killed or hurt, just as long as they get their timber out. Tim would still be alive if they cared. He was the one who always told them the chute was unsafe." The boy was close to tears again.

Meg put her hand on his, trying to reassure him. "The union's the only thing that can help us now, John."

For a long time they talked about all the things that had happened to them since they had decided to come to shanty. Tim's death showed them how completely powerless they had been, but it also gave them the resolve to do something about it.

Cameron reacted to Tim's death like one in torment. In spite of his aching leg he stayed with the injured men all through the night, tending their wounds and comforting them when they woke. It was as if he held himself personally responsible for Tim's death, and he wanted to punish himself for his negligence. Mrs. Ferguson pleaded with him to rest, and she had to get Jacques to force him to sit down so she could examine his injured leg, but he would only sit for a moment.

Grief gripped everyone in the shanty. They were quiet, trying not to disturb the injured men, pondering the meaning of Tim's death, and although they did not speak about it, they were all obsessed by the problem of what they should do next. It was a strange mood. The shantymen appeared passive and depressed, unable to rouse themselves out of their lethargy, but under the surface their anger festered away, ready to explode into action.

The day after the accident the men did not go out to work. Early in the morning Jacques organized a small group to cut pine boards with rip saws to make a coffin for the body. Another group took shovels, picks and axes up the hill behind the shanty to dig a grave out of the frozen ground. After working most of the morning they had hacked a hole about four feet deep. It would be enough to keep the wolves away until the spring, when the ground would be thawed enough to dig a proper grave.

By the late afternoon all the preparations had been completed, and the men gathered in the camboose shanty to honour their dead friend. There was no one to conduct a service in the wilderness. The body could not be sent back to Ireland, and Tim had no relatives in Canada. The men would do the ceremony themselves and bury their friend here, in the Algonquin Highlands, the country he had learned to love.

There was no table in the camboose shanty and the coffin was laid on the floor near the door. The forty shantymen sat on the benches, deep in their own thoughts. A fire blazed in the camboose, breaking the silence of the room whenever the wood sparked and hissed, and a candle made out of pork fat and string flickered in a tin plate at the head of the coffin, where a crude wooden cross had been laid. Finally, Jacques broke the silence with a simple eulogy.

"Tim was our friend and now he is dead. We remember him as a hot-tempered man who would bow to no one, and we came to love and respect him for what he was. He learned his work like few others in the shanties. I know of no one who could handle a horse in the bush as well as him. I'll remember him for being brave when the rest of us around him were cowards. I'll remember him as a true and loyal friend and my sorrow will not easily be forgotten."

Jacques stopped talking as abruptly as he began. The group huddled around the casket, waiting for someone else to speak. Then Cameron began in a soft voice that gave an intensity and depth of feeling to his words.

"We stand condemned by Tim's death. More than any other man in this shanty he wanted us to do something about working conditions and particularly the log chute. All of us, but myself more than any other, resisted Tim's demands. We said let's wait. We're not strong enough. Things will change. We'll win if we're patient. But things did not change, and the log chute got more dangerous the higher it grew, and then it collapsed, and Tim, the very person who wanted to do something about it, was crushed and killed underneath. We must live with our consciences. I must live with mine. We all killed him, just as surely as we argued to do nothing about the chute."

A number of other men spoke in turn about Tim, and what he meant to them as a person, and how they felt about his death. Some of the speeches were disjointed, and others were simple and direct, but all were spoken with conviction and meaning. Finally, the speeches were over. Two of the men got up and removed the lid of the coffin so that they **were** able to see Tim for the last time.

He was dressed in his rough work clothes, the only belongings he had with him and his hands were folded across his chest. The side of his head that had been crushed was covered with a piece of white canvas, but the rest of his face had a white, ghostly look about it. The lips were blue, and the eyes had a sunken hollow look about them. It was Tim, but the body was only a pale memory of the vigorous man they had known only a day before.

After a few moments of silence the shantymen replaced the lid of the coffin and nailed it firmly shut. Six men came forward, lifted the box, and took it outside. Then they hoisted it onto their shoulders and started climbing the hill behind the shanty. The men formed in pairs behind the pallbearers, and the procession wound its way up to the spot where the grave had been dug.

From the gravesite they could see out across the whole landscape. The storm had blown itself out, leaving a foot of powdery white snow. It was cold, well below zero, but a weak sun slanted out of a pale blue sky. Beneath them the snowcovered surface of Cache

Lake reflected the soft glare of the sun, and in the distance the dark wooded hills stood against the horizon.

They lowered the coffin into the ground with ropes, and stood for what seemed like a long time around the grave. Then Cameron took a shovel and emptied dirt onto the top of the coffin. "We swear we will not forget you," he said with conviction. Others took the shovel in turn, until the grave was covered.

The serious mood did not alter once the men were back in the shanty, but they seemed more optimistic. The funeral had given them the opportunity to express themselves openly about Tim's death, and now that it was over they felt better. Cameron saw it was time for decisive action. "Call the unionists together," he said to John, who was standing by his side. "We need a meeting."

In a moment the small group made up of Cameron, Jacques, Mrs. Ferguson, Meg and John had assembled. Cameron was deadly serious. "What are we going to do about Tim's death? I think now's the time for action. What do the rest of you think?"

"I think we should stop work until Hardy meets some of our demands," said Meg.

"Go on strike? Do you really think so?" Jacques seemed undecided.

"Yes," replied Cameron. "We could strike for better working conditions. That's one issue. And we could try and get the union recognized so that we could operate openly without the fear of getting fired."

"And no more fines," piped up John. The others smiled to see it was him that made this suggestion.

But Jacques was still cautious. "We've got to be careful. We've got no idea what Hardy or MacInnes will do."

"It's interesting they didn't come to the funeral. That shows what they think of us. They don't care who gets killed. It could be Angus, could be Tim, it could be any one of us, and they wouldn't care. We've got to defeat them before they kill us all."

"I don't know, Cameron. Hardy's tough and Mac-Innes is crafty. There's no telling what they'll do. We'd be better off waiting until Percy comes up in the spring. Then we could negotiate directly with him. Hardy could force us out into the snow with no food, or maybe blacklist us all and then we'd never get another job."

"But don't you see, Jacques? We have to do something," said Cameron desperately. "We've talked long enough, and now look what happened to Tim. If we'd taken some action on the log chute he'd still be with us. The men expect us to do something, and we have to do it now or we fail them." Cameron's feeling of guilt made him determined to carry out some act of revenge. His pale blue eyes gleamed with intensity. "If we don't act now then we'll never have the strength to act again." He paused, searching Jacques' face for any hint of opposition.

"I agree then, Cameron. We can't wait any longer."

"Good. Now, before we do anything let's talk to the others to get their opinions."

The unionists circulated among the others, talking quietly about their plans. Within a few moments they were back reporting in excited whispers that every man, without exception, favoured a strike. Cameron strode to the centre of the shanty and addressed the men.

"Men ... men the time has come when we must act! We have seen what this company will do to us. We have seen hardship. We have seen that the company men have no regard for our safety. We have seen two of our friends, two of the best among us, killed working for this company. We have seen ourselves abused and ignored. Now is the time to change all of that! Now is the time to stand up for ourselves. Now is the time to strike so that we can get what we deserve!" It was a fierce speech. Cameron paused. The men waited breathlessly for him to continue. "I say we should go on strike. What are your feelings?"

"Yes! Yes!" the shantymen shouted as one person.

"Is there any opposition?" There was silence.

"Then we are agreed that we go on strike, and this is what we strike for. We want a say in the running of the camp and particularly in the safety precautions. We want our union recognized, and no blacklistings because a person's in the union. And we want no more fines. Do we all agree?" To a man they shouted their agreement. "So it's settled. We go out on strike and we'll stay out as long as it takes to win these demands."

Cameron sat down with a piece of paper and pencil. Carefully he wrote down all the demands and concluded by stating they would strike until these demands were met. Then each person in the shanty signed their name at the bottom to attest to their agreement with the document. When it was finished Mrs. Ferguson was delegated to deliver it to the company men. It was supper time when she returned and the men lined up around the camboose with their plates.

Suddenly, without warning, Hardy and MacInnes came through the door of the shanty, each carrying a weapon. Hardy held a Winchester lever-action rifle, and MacInnes carried a heavy double-barrelled shotgun. The hard, black, shiny barrels of the guns gleamed in the camboose fire as they moved restlessly from man to man, pointing directly at vulnerable chests and stomachs. The faces of the two company men seemed threatening: each mouth was turned down in a frightening scowl, their jaws were set, their eyes watching carefully as if they were ready for the worst.

"All right," shouted Hardy, a brittle edge to his voice. "You men put that food down!" They stared at him in shock. It took a moment to comprehend, but Hardy's desperate look convinced them of his seriousness. He waved his rifle and shouted "You heard me! Put that food down!"

Cameron and Jacques stood up to meet them. "What are the guns for, Hardy?" asked Cameron, trying to keep calm.

"We're protecting the company property!" said Hardy, training his rifle on Cameron's chest.

"Don't point those guns. Someone might get hurt."

A half smile came over Hardy's face as he saw the terror of the men. "Look, you're not working for the company now that you're on strike. That food you're eating is company food, and men who don't work for the company don't have any right to eat it. This shanty belongs to the company, and you can get out of it and stay out as long as you're on strike!"

Hardy's huge frame towered over the men. The rifle pointed from man to man, ready to explode. MacInnes stood by his side, dwarfed by the big shotgun, a crazy smile on his face as if he was enjoying the fear of the men. All the shantymen were speechless.

Hardy shouted again. "I want you to put that food down! No man eats again unless he comes back and works for the company. And I want you out of this shanty. No man sleeps here unless he works for the Percy Lumber Company, and if you're on strike that means you don't work for us any more. You shantymen understand that and understand it well!" He paused for a moment, letting the impact of his words sink in. "We'll take any man who wants to come back to work, all you have to do is ask, but if you're on strike then you get out into the snow and stay there."

"You can't do that!" said Cameron.

"Can't I, now? Any man can protect his property, and that's all I'm doing."

The men looked at Cameron, but he was uncertain of his next move.

Hardy spoke again, his voice threatening and scornful, a hint of madness about it. "You men have to learn that I'm the one with power in this shanty and what I say goes. Nobody else matters ... understand that! If you want any food and if you want a place to sleep tonight then I say forget about this strike. But if you want to carry on, then get out into the snow and stay there forever!"

Again the shantymen waited for Cameron to act, but what could he do? The company men had the guns to enforce their will. If they dared resist there was no telling what action Hardy would take.

John and Meg stood in the background with the others. Something had to be done. Hardy had to be opposed, or the strike would collapse and the union with it. Impulsively, John drew attention to himself. "You think you're so important, Hardy," he said with bravado. "We'll go out into the snow, but you can't defeat us and don't think that you can! But before I go out I'm going to have my supper."

The boy went to the camboose, took a tin plate and ladled out a healthy portion of beans. He tore off some bread from a loaf and was about to dip his cup into the tea when suddenly the rifle exploded. The bullet slammed into the corduroy floor a foot in front of him. John's plate dropped to the ground, spilling the beans onto his work pants. He was terrified.

For a moment the shock of the explosion stunned everyone. Men were on their feet, knives in their hands, ready to strike. Bloodshed hung in the air. One false move would have left two dead company men.

Cameron forcibly reasserted his leadership. "That wasn't necessary, Hardy!" he shouted. "We'll have no shootings in this strike! We'll leave your shanty and your food, and we'll wait in the bush until you agree to our demands. But let me tell you this. If there's any more killings in this camp I'll guarantee your safety no longer!"

CHAPTER 11

A S the men got ready to go out into the night, they swore under their breath. Hardy's tactics were unfair. Everyone had known there were guns in the camp: they were needed for protection in case of prowling wolves or bears. But it had not occurred to anyone that Hardy would turn the guns against them. It was one more indignity for them to bear. They would show him, they thought; they would stay out on strike so long that eventually the company would be brought to its knees and Hardy would beg them to come back to finish the season's work.

But as soon as they got outside that mood of defiance changed into doubt and anxiety. The storm had been followed by a midwinter cold spell that plunged the temperatures well below zero. A pale sliver of a moon shone out of the east, the sky was filled with thousands of glittering stars, and the northern lights shimmered in weird patterns of blue, green, and silver. The crisp new-fallen snow squeaked under their feet as they trudged up the hill behind the camp. They pulled their hats over their ears and hunched into their clothes, but in time the cold crept across their shoulders and numbed their feet.

Cameron walked with the men, limping badly from the injury he had received when the log chute collapsed. He seemed withdrawn, staring at the ground as he walked, his shoulders slouched in an attitude of despair. His mackinaw hung open in spite of the cold, his long hair was dishevelled, and his usual self-confidence was gone. He pondered the sudden turn of events, feeling the burden of his responsibility.

No one had to ask what was going on in his mind. The shantymen had been outmanoeuvred. For some reason no one had had the foresight to think what would happen once they were on strike. They just assumed that they would stop working and stay in the shanty until the issue was resolved. It was as if Tim's death had swept them into a course of action without clearly knowing where it would lead them.

They busied themselves to keep up their spirits. When they got to the top of the hill they set to work building fires to keep out the bitter cold. They tried to reassure themselves that what they had done was right and that in time they would win the strike.

"We'll show Hardy and MacInnes," one of the younger shantymen said. "They'll give in. They can't put up with a strike for long. They need us to build the log chute or they'll never get the timber downriver, and that'll break the company."

"Yeah," said another. "I want to get that Hardy so bad! And MacInnes! The way they treat us you'd think we're dogs. We'll show them this time."

"All we have to do is stick together, and they can't do nothing to us."

This was more brave talk than good sense. Once the fires were started Cameron moved off by himself to brood about their predicament. Meg, John, Mrs. Ferguson and Jacques met briefly together. Jacques assumed leadership in Cameron's absence, "We've got to move among the men to keep up spirits. Don't let them get defeated."

It was to no avail. Slowly the shantymen became depressed and suggestions of defeat crept into their conversations. The cold was piercing, and in spite of the roaring fires the shantymen constantly had to move about, shuffling their feet, and clasping and unclasping their hands so they would not freeze. As the night wore on everyone became tired, and hunger made them short-tempered. Gradually conversations came to an end and each man turned inward, trying to make up his mind what to do next.

"What can we do?" Meg asked when she found John. "I heard some men talking that we shouldn't have gone out on strike."

John agreed. "Seems like some of them want to give up."

Together they sought out Jacques and Mrs. Ferguson. "We must do something," said Meg. "The men are talking of deserting us."

The Canadien nodded. "I agree, but what can we do?"

Mrs. Ferguson whispered so that just the four of them could hear. "We've got to have some action. We must show the shantymen that we aren't defeated. Now, I know that in the wood shed there's canvas and food. I say we should go down and get it."

"But what about Hardy and the guns?" asked Jacques. "If we act swiftly he'll know nothing about it until it's too late."

The four of them went over to Cameron to discuss their plans, but the union leader shrugged his shoulders as if he had already resigned himself to defeat.

Mrs. Ferguson reacted angrily. "What is it, Cameron? We must do something or the men will lose heart, and the strike will be finished."

"Yes, you're right." But the mood of defeat still hung heavily on his words.

"I think the cook's right," said Jacques. "If we're quick we can get the food and canvas and then Hardy can't get it back even with his guns."

Jacques started to organize the raid. "You'll have to stay here, Cameron. Your leg's too bad to go down the hill."

"I'll come," said John eagerly.

"Me too," added Meg.

"No!" said Cameron with sudden forcefulness. "Those two Bain kids are not to take any risks."

"But why not?" said Meg, feeling hurt.

"Your family has given too much already, Meg. You're not to take any more risks."

"Yes ... yes that's right," said the cook. "Anyway, we need you two here." In spite of their protests John and Meg were overruled.

Jacques and Mrs. Ferguson rehearsed the plans for the raid over and over until they were satisfied. Then they called a group of men together and carefully went over it with them, Five men were to go down the hill towards the shanty, talking loudly to attract attention.

Three more would circle around through the bush, and, as the others diverted attention, they would slip into the woodshed and take out the canvas tarpaulins and a half-empty hogshead of pork. They talked for a long time, refining every detail, pointing out from the hill where each group should be and at what time, and then finally they were ready.

The three men left to circle around through the bush to be in a good position to go into the shed. They were the biggest and strongest men in the shanty, chosen so they could bring out the provisions as fast as possible. The five men stood on the hill waiting tensely until finally, with a wave of a hand signalling that they were in position, the five men headed down the hill.

The two shanties were quiet, not a sound, not a light, not an indication of movement. The rest of the men on the hill strained to see what was happening in the light of the pale moon. The group went down the hill, talking loudly. The three men in the bush waited to make their move, and then, finally, as the others got into position, they started for the shed.

The rifle from the foreman's shanty exploded. The men could see the long flash in the dark coming from the muzzle of the gun. The two groups hesitated for a moment, then the men all turned to run for cover in the bush. The rifle fired again and then again; the explosions splitting the quiet of the still night, the red flashes blazing out of the muzzle of the gun. Men ran for their lives out of sheer terror, tumbling and clawing to get into the protection of the bush. Then there was silence.

Slowly the men straggled back to the fires. No one had been injured, no one even knew if Hardy had been aiming his rifle. All they knew was that they had been discovered and had been forced to turn tail and run.

For a long time they stood around the fire, recounting the events of the shooting. They complained bitterly that Hardy had used the gun on them, but it confirmed their belief that both of the company men were willing to go to any lengths to defeat them. Gradually as the night wore on the shantymen grew silent.

They tried to keep busy. Groups of men took torches and hunted in the bush for more wood to burn, but most still huddled around the fire. The cold penetrated their clothing. Gradually it became a grim struggle for survival. It was hard to keep enough firewood to stay warm. They were all hungry, and this made them even more short-tempered, and they were so tired some of them had to be shaken every few minutes to keep from falling asleep.

In time the shantymen came to realize they were defeated. They joined Cameron sitting glumly by the fire, and stared vacantly into the glowing coals, trying to decide what to do next. John, Meg, Mrs. Ferguson and Jacques moved around trying to keep up spirits, but they were ignored.

There were faint grey streaks in the east when the first of the men went back to the camboose shanty. Four men who had been sitting together suddenly got to their feet and began walking down the hill towards the shanty. Meg ran after them. "Don't go!" she shouted desperately. "We can win if we stay together!" But the men did not even look back. They hunched into their clothes as if to avoid the girl and continued downhill.

Meg ran in desperation back to Cameron. "A group of men are heading back to the shanty! We've got to stop them!"

Cameron did nothing. For just a moment he glanced up at her and smiled gently and then looked back into the fire. The look conveyed the message clearly. They had been defeated and all hope was gone.

The men settled back in front of the fire, but a few minutes later another group got up and headed back to the shanty. Meg felt she had to try to stop them, but Cameron's firm grip on her shoulder held her in place. Then another group got up, and then another, and then finally all of the shantymen were going back downhill. They were silent, watching their feet as they shuffled through the snow, but there was no mistaking it; they were defeated men.

The unionists were the only ones left by the fire now. They sat for a few minutes without speaking. Cameron's face was lined with strain. His quiet blue eyes seemed sunk deep in his face; he was an enigma, his face a mask covering his emotions. Jacques stirred restlessly, rubbing his hands together as if he could barely contain himself. Mrs. Ferguson stared into the fire, a look of complete resignation on her face. The defeat gave John and Meg a new sense of urgency. They had to find a way of defeating the company men.

Slowly Cameron got to his feet. He kicked snow into the fire to extinguish the last of the flames and then quietly announced, "It's time for us to go." Without another word he headed down the hill, still limping badly from his leg injury. The others joined him on either side. They went in slow procession down the hill to face the victorious company men.

Hardy and MacInnes suddenly appeared out of the foreman's shanty, guns in hand. Men poured out of the camboose shanty to witness the showdown. Hardy could barely contain his anger; his mouth was turned into a hard scowl; the scar on his cheek was a vivid red. MacInnes stood beside him dancing restlessly as he held the heavy shotgun. He seemed overjoyed at the prospect of defeating the men.

"Where are you going?" Hardy shouted, his rifle pointing menacingly at Cameron's chest. MacInnes' shotgun moved nervously from person to person. For a long time no one spoke. The unionists were frozen into position as if waiting for the guns to explode.

"Turn those guns away," said Cameron, keeping his emotions in tight control.

"I'll not!" Hardy shouted. "You're to get out of my shanty!"

"You said anyone could come back to work. We've come back just like the others."

"Listen to him," said MacInnes in his high-pitched voice. "You'd think Cameron ran this shanty."

"You need all the men you can get to finish the log chute by spring break-up."

"Not you, Cameron, and not those Bains kids either. You're all troublemakers. Jacques, he can come back and so can Mrs. Ferguson, but not the rest of you. You're only here to start a union, and I'll not put up with it!"

"You gave your word, Hardy! You said everyone could come back who wanted to come back!"

"I know your doings, Cameron. I've seen it coming from the beginning of the season. And that boy and girl. They're just like their father, always causing trouble. You're finished in the shanties. I'll see to it that none of you ever work in the bush again. You'll be blacklisted and no timber company in the Ottawa Valley will ever hire you!" As Hardy shouted, his gun never wavered from Cameron. There was no doubt that he was ready to impose his will by force if necessary.

"You can't do that," said Jacques, his voice trembling with rage. "They've done nothing."

"They led a strike against the company," said Mac-Innes, barely containing his joy. "They'll have to pay for it. Let them walk back down the Opeongo Line; let them see what it's like when there isn't a company to protect them!"

"We can't let them do that," said Jacques appealing to the other shantymen circling around. "They are our leaders, Cameron is our leader, and the others are just kids — and Angus Bains' kids at that. They must stay!"

"No!" shouted Hardy in a huge, angry voice. "They go! They have been organizing against us! They must go!"

"That's not fair!" shouted Jacques. "We cannot let it happen … "

"Stop!" shouted Cameron, interrupting Jacques in mid-sentence. "Stop before it leads to something we cannot control!" The union leader suddenly turned away from the others, showing his back to them. He held his fingers lightly against his temples as if trying to shut everything out so he could concentrate. Then finally he turned slowly back to face the guns. His face was ashen white, his eyes were fixed firmly on Hardy, his tight control gave a hard brittle quality to his voice.

"You have won this time, Hardy. If we try and use violence to defeat you then you will use the guns against us and say it was our fault. But we'll remember this day, Hardy, and we'll remember Angus Bains, and we'll remember Tim, and we'll remember all the things that have happened this season, and some day you will have to reckon with it. We are not going to give up. Let everyone remember that. We are going to defeat you eventually even if it takes years to do it. That's a promise."

For a moment they were silent, each staring angrily at the other, and then a cruel smile came across Hardy's face. "You're finished, Cameron. You'll get out of my shanty. You and that boy and girl fix yourself some breakfast and then get out and don't come back. None of you will ever work in the shanties again. Remember that! You'll never win the union!"

CHAPTER 12

CAMERON, John and Meg walked south from the shanty, skirting the islands in the middle of Cache Lake, and then down the long south bay until they came to the beginning of the tote road. They were tired. Each of them felt they had enough strength to get through the day, but they set a slow pace to conserve energy. The temperature was well below zero, but the sun was shining brightly out of a pale blue sky, giving warmth as it reflected off the snow.

They had prepared carefully for the long trip down the Opeongo Line. They carried canvas duffle bags slung over their shoulders that contained all of their belongings and a little food. John had pushed a light axe into his bag just in case there was trouble. They were dressed warmly in long winter underwear, heavy woollen trousers and mackinaws, and each wore their snowshoes.

The scene at breakfast had been difficult. The men felt so defeated they had acted in a confused way. Many of them sat as far away from John, Meg and Cameron as they were able, trying to avoid listening to them. Others wished them a good trip but in a very formal way, betraying their discomfort. It was as if their presence was a reminder that the strike had been a failure.

When Hardy came into the shanty and ordered them back to work, the men seemed relieved to get away.

Only Jacques and Mrs. Ferguson were there to see them off. The cook bent over to kiss John and Meg. She would miss their good humour and hard work. Jacques shook hands with the three of them. He searched for something to say, but was at a loss for words. What would the rest of the season be like without them? But there was nothing to be done. Hardy was now in undisputed control of the shanty. When they finally were on the trail it was like a great relief, now their only worry was making it to the next stopping place before sunset.

When they got to the end of the south bay they found the first slash on a tree indicating the start of the tote road. It was a steep climb from the lake shore to the crest of the ridge, and Cameron was limping badly. John led the way carefully, choosing the easiest trail and setting a slow pace so Cameron could keep up. Once they had made it to the top of the grade the tote road followed a series of winding ridges. Meg and John walked out in front, setting a faster pace. They had to be certain they would get to the stopping place on Lawrence Lake before nightfall.

The scenery was beautiful. The new fallen-snow hung on the branches of the dark evergreens, sparkling in the bright sunshine. Rabbit tracks were everywhere, and they passed the trail of a fox who had struggled through the snow, looking for the buds of maple trees to feed on. The birds were everywhere. A flock of large black ravens followed in the crowns of trees, waiting for them to leave something to eat. The jays were the noisiest, chattering as if they constantly had news to repeat to one another. Once from the top of a hill they saw the form of the Arctic owl far in the distance over Cache Lake, keeping its lonely vigil as it slowly circled the lake in search for food. Both John and Meg felt pangs of regret that they were leaving this wild country and its harsh beauty.

There were few large trees left along the trail. Last season the men of Percy's Company had been stationed at the shanty on Harness Lake and they had cut over this area. The stumps were enormous, some of them were over six feet in diameter; the trees had been 150 feet high. All of the companies seemed to think that the Ottawa River Valley was so rich in stands of timber that it would never be depleted. Every year they took out only the best trees for the squared timber trade, and every year they were forced to go further and further back into the headwaters of the tributaries of the Ottawa until it seemed inevitable that soon the best of the timber would be gone. No one wanted to think of that day; their goal was to cut timber as cheaply and as quickly as possible and let the future worry about itself.

Meg and John walked side by side, often chatting about what they saw or the events of the last few days. In spite of their exhaustion from lack of sleep both were remarkably strong for their age. The time they had spent in the shanty had agreed with them, toughening them both mentally and physically, and now they were able to withstand the rigours of the Algonquin Highlands as well as any shantyman.

They were deep in conversation when Meg happened to glance around and found that Cameron was not behind them. They stopped and waited, but everything was still. All they could hear was the noisy chatter of a jay somewhere far off in the bush. Five minutes went by, but still Cameron did not appear. They began retracing their steps, walking hurriedly in case there was some trouble. Both of them were beginning to panic when they found Cameron painfully making his way, limping heavily on his injured leg.

"Your leg's bad," John said. "Are you in a lot of pain, Cameron?" His worry was communicated in the tone of his voice.

Cameron leaned against a tree, taking the weight off his leg. He did not speak for some time, but seemed to be collecting his strength and waiting for the pain to subside. Behind his reddish beard his face was white and the exhaustion and strain etched deep lines around his eyes and mouth. Finally, he replied, "The pain seems to get worse with the walking."

Like a lot of working men, Cameron rarely complained. Such a terse statement meant the pain was bad, maybe very bad. They stood quietly for a moment, but the same thought was with them all. They were facing a 150-mile walk down the Opeongo Line. How could they manage if Cameron's leg was so badly injured? Finally, John asked quietly. "Maybe we should go back to the Cache Lake shanty?"

"We can't go back," said Cameron emphatically. "I won't go back and be beholden to Hardy. I'll be all right. Let's press on and make the Lawrence Lake Stopping Place before sunset."

They said nothing, but both John and Meg were worried.

Cameron was a big man and he would be impossible to carry if his leg gave out. Even if they got to Lawrence Lake they had little money. The operators of stopping places were notoriously tight-fisted about giving credit. What would happen if they were forced to spend three or four days waiting for Cameron's leg to get better? But still, going back to Cache Lake seemed impossible. There was nothing to do but to carry on in the hope that he would get stronger.

After a few minutes rest they set out again. John cut Cameron a staff for support, but the snow was so deep it was of little use. Meg took his pack and walked beside him, but because the snowshoes were in the way she could not even help support him. They doggedly struggled along until in the early afternoon they came down out of the hills onto Harness Lake. The wind had blown much of the loose snow off the ice and Cameron was able to use the staff much more effectively. When they caught sight of the deserted camboose shanty John plunged on ahead to light a fire, leaving Cameron and Meg to come behind.

By the time they caught up, he had a fire roaring on the camboose and was melting snow for tea in a small kettle he was carrying. Cameron sat on a bench close to the fire and almost immediately dozed off. They had been continuously out of doors for hours, and it sapped their energy just to generate enough body heat to keep warm.

Meg arranged bread close to the fire so it would thaw out, and put some slices of salt pork into a skillet to fry. As they worked, the two of them watched the sleeping Cameron. They had known him as such a strong, determined man that it was difficult to imagine he was badly injured. Both of them had the same unspoken anxiety. Would they be able to make it down the Opeongo Line with a man who could barely walk?

No sooner had they finished their lunch than Cameron got to his feet and prepared to go. John hesitated. "Maybe we should stay here for the night? At least we would be warm and it would give a chance to rest your leg."

"Let's push on. This place would be hard to heat. It's only a few miles on to Lawrence Lake. My leg'll hold out till then. When we get there we can sleep in warm beds and eat a hot meal. Maybe we'll spend an extra day there while I rest."

They agreed, but they had not gone far when John and Meg wondered about the wisdom of that decision. Cameron limped badly, but there was little either of them could do to help. They tried letting him walk with his arm over one of their shoulders, but the snowshoes got in the way. John thought of making a toboggan out of saplings but he had nothing to bind them together. Cameron had to be left to struggle along as best he could.

They became more and more concerned. It was getting later in the afternoon and they had little reserve energy. But there was no going back. They were some distance away from the Harness Lake shanty, and it seemed better to press on and try and make it to the Lawrence Lake Stopping Place. The trip was no longer a pleasant escape from the shanty. It had become a nightmare all of its own.

The sun was little more than three-quarters of an hour from dipping behind the hill, and the shadows were lengthening in the bush. Soon it would be too dark to find the slashes on the trail. John went a long way in front, hoping to find the road leading towards Lawrence Lake, but it followed the top of the ridge without a hint that they were close to the lake.

He kept glancing at the sun, carefully calculating how much sunlight was left. Finally, when there was less than a quarter of an hour till sunset and still no sign of the lake, he knew they were not going to make it. It was too late to go back to Harness Lake, and it was too much of a risk to try to follow an unknown trail with an injured man after nightfall. They were trapped in the bush for the night.

John knew what had to be done. He hurried on ahead, following the tote road, looking for some kind of shelter. He came to a thicket of white birches; they would give some protection but they still seemed open and exposed. He pushed on a hundred yards more until he found what he was looking for. Just to the north of the trail there was a sheer rock face rising some thirty feet and about fifty yards wide. It was not high, but it was steep enough to keep the wind off their backs. The other advantage was that it looked south and would get the last rays of sun that evening and the first rays the next morning. At least this would give some protection.

Once he struggled up to the rock face John dumped his packs onto the ground. He was so tired his shoulders ached and his legs seemed rubbery. All he wanted to do was collapse in the snow and sleep forever, but there was no time to be wasted. Their survival depended on the preparation for the night ahead.

He kicked off his snowshoes and used one of them as a shovel to clear away a six-foot square at the base of the rock face. The snow was over three feet deep, and after he scraped it down to the dirt it made a bank which would surround them once they crouched in the spot that had been cleared. They could sit with their backs to the rock face and have a fire to their front. It would make them low, and out of the wind, and the snow would reflect the heat towards them. Maybe that would keep enough warmth to survive the night.

John stood up from his labours and noticed the others struggling along the tote road a hundred yards away. "Cameron! Meg!" he shouted "Over here!" He put on his snowshoes and ran to give them help.

The shantyman was exhausted. He limped so badly that he barely seemed to make any progress. His weathered face was lined with exhaustion and worry, and his reddish beard was full of hoar frost around his mouth. "Glad to see you, boy. For a moment I thought you'd deserted us."

Meg and John helped Cameron over to the rock face as best they could, but they would not let him sit. The warmth of his body would melt the snow and dampen his trousers. Later they would freeze and he would be uncomfortable.

John took his axe and trimmed the branches off a small hemlock tree close by. He hauled them back to the campsite and carefully arranged them around the base of the rock face, in a thick mat, immediately behind the place where he would light the fire. Then Meg eased Cameron into place.

Their work was far from finished. The sun would set within minutes, and the light was already quickly fading. They would have to get an enormous pile of firewood or by morning they would be frozen. John took the axe and went out searching for firewood. Meg collected some dead branches from a small pine tree, then found a rotting maple a couple of inches in thickness, and hauled them back to the campsite. Taking out her knife she cut one of the dry sticks into long, paper-thin shavings. She lit these, and then added small twigs and larger sticks until it was a roaring fire. Leaving the fire for Cameron to tend, she headed back into the bush to find more wood.

The sun was set and it would be a clear night. The temperature would plunge well below zero before sunrise. John and Meg worked frantically. Most of the dead wood lay buried under the snow, and they had to rely on dead branches that were within easy reach. John lopped them off with his axe as quickly as he could and Meg hauled them back to the fire. Then he found another dead maple about four inches in diameter. He cut it down, chopped it into three sections, and Meg dragged it back to camp. They headed out in another direction and found two more dead trees. This time the two of them had to wrestle them to the fire. They returned again and again to find more and more firewood, and the pile grew larger and larger. Finally, Meg found a large dead poplar tree about a hundred yards from the fire. John chopped it down and cut it into pieces. By the time he had finished hauling it to the fire it was so dark they could not find their way around the bush any longer.

Both of them kicked off their snowshoes and settled on the hemlock boughs beside Cameron. It was almost warm and cozy there by the fire, out of the piercing cold of the evening air. The snow embankment and the rock face reflected the heat and held a small pocket of warmth where the three of them were crouched. Cameron had taken the food out of the tote bags and left it to thaw by the fire. He had filled the kettle with snow and already the water was close to boiling. Meg found the small package of tea and threw what was left of it into the kettle. They ate their meal of salt pork ravenously, and then washed it down with tea. As a final preparation they took out all of their spare clothing and put it on, They would need as much warmth as they could find to survive the night.

There was nothing more to be done. Cameron took out his pipe, stuffed it with tobacco from a small package he carried, and lit it with a stick from the fire. The exhaustion of the shantyman seemed complete. His eyes were hooded by heavy swollen eyelids, his mouth was pulled tight with strain, and every movement was exaggerated as if it took all his effort and concentration.

They sat in silence for a long time and then finally John spoke. "It was a mistake for us to leave the Cache Lake shanty with you in such bad shape, Cameron."

The shantyman drew thoughtfully on his pipe. "There was nothing more to be done. We lost the strike."

John nodded in agreement.

"I blame myself for the loss." Cameron's voice seemed hollow and empty. "We should have known

Hardy would use guns. We were too impatient. We should have waited for Percy to come in the spring like Jacques suggested. Now the union is finished and all the hopes of the men are gone."

"But we can get help. There's unions in Ottawa and Montreal and Toronto. They'll help us."

Cameron shook his head. "We have to do it ourselves. By the time we get to Ottawa and get organized the season'll be over, and we've lost our chance. All we've accomplished is to get ourselves blacklisted from the shanties."

Meg leaned forward. "Don't give up, Cameron. Things will look better in the morning."

"Aye, that may be true." Cameron's feelings of defeat seemed complete. Not only was the union shattered, and with it all his efforts for the last few months, but even his physical strength had been drained. There was nothing more to be said; events would have to work out by themselves.

One person would have to be awake at all times through the night to tend the fire and make sure hands and feet did not freeze. Cameron was so exhausted that he put up no resistance when John and Meg volunteered to take the first shift. The shantyman lay down on the mattress of hemlock boughs, and within a moment he was fast asleep.

John and Meg arranged their tote bags behind Cameron and then built up the fire. They both were so exhausted they had to concentrate on staying awake. There was little left to do except tend the fire and arrange the wood so that it would be within easy reach. Periodically they checked their hands and feet to see that they were not freezing, and made sure that Cameron was comfortable.

The time passed slowly. They could peer out of the hole they had made in the snow and see the stars above and the trees faintly stirring in the wind, but that was all. Somewhere an owl made low hooting sounds, and far off in the distance they heard the yelping of wolves out on hunt. Both of them shivered. That would be the same pack they had heard the night they had come into the shanty on this very trail. It seemed so long ago.

"What will we do when we get home, John?" Meg suddenly asked.

"I don't know. We'll have to get a job somewhere." John was quiet for a few moments. "It seems so unfair, Meg. I mean, we weren't doing anything different from anyone else. Why did he have to fire us? You know, I think Hardy never wanted us in the shanty. Right from the time when we first met him in Mr. Percy's office I felt he was against us."

"It was 'cause he knew we'd be like father and stand up to him."

"Yes, I guess that's what it was." said John thoughtfully. They were quiet again, and then Meg said suddenly, "Maybe it was more than that."

"What do you mean?"

"When you think about it, it just makes sense that Hardy killed our father."

"Do you really believe that, Meg?"

"What else could it be? Dad was the union organizer, and everyone said that he brought the men together like no one else had done before. Hardy and MacInnes would know that. They figure everything out.

They tried to stop him and when they couldn't they murdered him."

"But we can't prove it, Meg. It sounds good but we have no proof."

"Why do we need proof. Hardy hated him, didn't he? And everyone says that there were a number of things they couldn't explain about Dad's death. What more proof do we need?"

"But it would never stand up in a court."

"Who needs a court? We know that he killed him. Isn't that enough?"

"But we can't prove it!"

Meg was exasperated with her brother. "Well I say we know who killed him and it wasn't an accident!"

"But Meg, don't you see? We can't accuse Hardy of something like that unless we can show that he did it."

"Then you end up doing nothing! You protect him!"

"I do not!" said John emphatically.

Meg folded her arms over her chest. It seemed so simple to her that she could not understand her brother's resistance. Now that she had figured out what had happened to their father, she was determined to do something about it. "We've got to go back to the shanty, John!" She said decisively.

"Why?"

"Hardy fired us so we'll never find out what happened to our father. I'm not going to stand for it. We're going back in the morning."

"But we can't do that. Hardy would never let us return."

"You just wait and see, John Bains. You just wait and see. Hardy's not going to get rid of us that easily."

"But Meg … "

"Don't but me, John!" she said. "I've decided! We'll get to the bottom of this!"

For a moment John was going to carry on with the argument, but then he sighed in resignation. He had learned long ago that there was no point in arguing with his younger sister when she had made up her mind. Maybe tomorrow things would be different and they could make some reasonable decision about what to do next. Now they were just too tired.

They stopped talking and listened to the sounds of the surrounding bush. Occasionally they could hear the wolves far to the north of them. The trees rustled restlessly in the light breeze. The fierce cold froze the bush solidly, but the three of them were snug within their pocket of warmth.

John stirred to put more wood on the fire and noticed that Meg had fallen asleep. He settled her gently against himself to share body warmth. His own weariness made him almost nod off to sleep several times, but he wanted to give Cameron as much rest as possible. Finally, he could keep his eyes open no longer, and woke the shantyman. Within moments of being relieved, John was asleep.

CHAPTER 13

THE next day broke calm, clear and cold. As the sun came over the horizon the dark sky gradually turned a pale blue and the light, slanting through the trees, gleamed on the crisp snow. It was the type of day when it felt good to be alive.

John and Meg awoke to the smell of salt pork frying in a skillet. Cameron was sitting beside the fire tending the food. He smiled in his old relaxed manner, the calm blue eyes and the set of his chin giving the impression that he was his normal, confident self again.

"Not much of a shantyman's breakfast," he said good-humouredly, nodding at the small pieces of pork, "but it beats eating the snow."

Meg smiled, "You look better, Cameron."

"I feel better. Much of the pain seemed to go when I had my sleep." He paused for a moment, tending the breakfast, and then he looked up and smiled at the two of them. "If it wasn't for you I doubt I would have made it through the night. I'm grateful."

Meg and John were pleased with the compliment. They passed the time while waiting for breakfast by chatting good-naturedly about the experiences of the trip and the previous night, but finally John could not put off the important question any longer. "How's your leg, Cameron?"

He seemed to search for an answer, delaying for a long time, and then he glanced up, smiling softly. "I'm afraid it's broken. I knew yesterday afternoon when the pain kept getting worse, but I didn't know how to tell the two of you. It needs to be set in splints and I shouldn't walk on it for a week or more."

For a long time the three of them silently pondered the alternatives, but the answer was clear. "We'll have to go back," John said. "We'll have to go back to the Cache Lake shanty to get help."

"Hardy will never let us back in the shanty, John. You know that. He'd rather see us dead first."

"We'll make him," said Meg. "We're going to go back because we figured out he was the one who killed our father. Isn't that right, John?"

"What's this?" asked Cameron.

"He killed our father and we're going back, or at least I'm going back, to catch him."

"But Meg, you can't prove it."

"It doesn't matter. I know he did it and I'm not going home until I settle it with him." Meg's determination surprised even Cameron. She seemed set in her course of action and no one could turn her from it.

"Anyway," said John. "Even if we wanted to go on we couldn't. It's a hundred and fifty miles down to Ottawa and your leg won't carry you. We've got almost no money and those innkeepers won't keep us for free."

Cameron said nothing. He had spent the night turning every possible alternative over in his mind. He wanted to hear how John and Meg viewed their predicament.

John went on. "The shantymen will just have to force Hardy to take us back. After all, you broke your leg working for the company. If he forces us out into the bush, he'd be killing us and the men won't stand for that."

Cameron stared into the fire. He was loathe to return to the camp and show Hardy that they were still dependent on him, but John was right. He knew that trying to carry on down the Opeongo Line was physically impossible.

"All right. We will have to hope that the shantymen will force Hardy to take us back."

Once they had made up their minds, they prepared quickly. They had much ground to cover, and they were tired from lack of food and the hours of continuous exposure to the cold Algonquin winter. After breakfast they covered the fire with snow, adjusted their packs and slipped on their snowshoes.

But as soon as Cameron put weight on his broken leg the pain shot up through his thigh into his chest and contorted his face. He tried to use the staff John had cut him the day before, but it was useless in the deep snow. After a lot of experimenting they finally discovered that the only way Cameron was able to move was for him to take the snowshoe off his injured leg, put his arm around either John or Meg's shoulder for support, and walk one-legged, holding the other above the snow.

It was an exhausting slow process that sapped the energy of all of them. Meg and John took turns supporting the shantyman, but they could hold the strain no longer than a hundred yards before they would have to rest. For almost two hours they kept at it until they reached the beginning of the hill leading down to Harness Lake.

Cameron called for a halt. "We'll have to split up," he said. "One of you will have to go on to Cache Lake for help. We will never make it like this." After some discussion it was agreed that John would go for help and Meg would stay with Cameron.

The shantyman gave very careful instructions. "Be careful, John. You're tired and it's important that you don't sit down to rest. You could fall asleep and then freeze to death. When you get to Cache Lake look for Jacques. He'll know what to do." After a brief farewell, John set off down the hill at a good pace.

Cameron and Meg struggled on again. They had to rest several times before they made it out onto the surface of the lake. Going across the ice, Meg thought several times that she would not be able to make it, but finally, pushed on by sheer determination, they made it to the deserted camboose shanty.

Cameron sat down on a bench beside the camboose and began setting a fire with small scraps of wood left over from yesterday. Meg went outside with the axe to collect enough firewood to see them through the rest of the day. The bush surrounding the shanty had been cleared of dead wood fit for burning the previous season and there was none left in the shed, so without a mo-ment's hesitation she went into the stable and began knocking down the wooden stalls that were still standing. This was no time to worry about destruction of property. It was an emergency, and they needed firewood in a hurry. Within minutes Meg had hauled and stacked more than a cord of wood. Once they had the fire blazing, the old shanty gradually warmed.

When John left the others he was feeling good. He walked down the hill with long strides and set off across the lake, thinking he would make it to Cache Lake within the hour, but it was not long before his exhaustion took its toll. By the time he made it to the other side of Harness Lake he was plodding slowly through the snow, forcing one foot after the other. When he got to the top of the first long hill all he wanted to do was sit down and rest. If it was not for Cameron's warning he might have done just that, but he forced himself on, step after step; until it seemed his walk would never end.

The cold frosted his breath, it pierced the lobes of his ears, and the tips of his fingers, but the sun reflecting off the snow made his face feel as if it was baking and the sweat trickled down between his shoulder blades. The trees passed and surrounded him, the jays called in piercing cries, the ravens cawed from the very tops of trees, and, high above, the snowy owl slowly circled his territory, looking for prey. John's legs were so tired that he seemed to be walking on wooden stilts, but he pressed on without a pause.

It felt as if hours had passed when the boy finally found himself going downhill, and he was out on the ice of Cache Lake. He was so tired that he decided to go down to the log chute rather than back to the shanty, because it was closer. Slowly he plodded across the lake until finally, close to collapse, he crested the hill and could see the shantymen working on the chute.

He staggered down the hill towards the confused mass of men. Some of them stopped working in surprise. "Look ... Look! It's Bains. John Bains!" The shouts went from man to man until everyone was downing their tools and tying up their animals. Within moments John was surrounded by anxious, questioning shantymen.

The emotional relief of getting back safely to the men so overwhelmed John that he had to sit down to collect his thoughts. They strained to piece together the broken sentences of the exhausted boy. "Cameron's leg ... it's broken ... he can't walk. We got caught in the bush last night before we could make it to the Lawrence Lake Stopping Place. We were outside all night. Meg and Cameron are back at the camboose shanty on Harness Lake. They're there now ... they've got no food. He can't walk ... they need help!"

It was Jacques who seized leadership. "I'll go and get him, John. Don't worry, we'll go right now."

"No! Let him stay at Harness Lake! Let him freeze! He doesn't work here any more!" It was Hardy: huge, angry, and ugly.

One of the younger shantymen turned on him, shouting threateningly. "We're going to get them, and we don't care what you say, Hardy!"

"What sort of a man are you?" shouted another.

"Murderer!" came an angry shout from the crowd.

Soon all the men were shouting at once in a sudden outpouring of pent-up hatred for Hardy and all the viciousness that he stood for. It reached a crescendo of anger, and Hardy dropped back in amazement, visibly shaken. Jacques calmly prepared to go. He and another young shantyman rigged a team of spirited horses, hitched them to a light sleigh and in a moment they set off at a gallop. Hardy did not dare to stop them.

John was taken back to the shanty, and after an enormous bowl of pork swimming in a delicious broth of beans, he climbed into his own warm cozy bunk and instantly fell asleep.

It was nightfall when he awoke. The men were pouring into the camboose shanty, stomping the snow off their boots and peeling off their scarfs and mackinaws. Their booming voices filled the room, and their wind-browned faces shone with good humour. John's return and the confrontation with Hardy had suddenly changed the mood of the camp from defeat to an optimistic sense of purpose.

John climbed out of his bunk and joined the line of men that had formed around the camboose, waiting their turn to serve themselves supper out of the big iron pots and kettles. He was the centre of attention. All of the men wanted to know about the hardships of the trail and how he was feeling from his ordeal. But more than seeking information, the talk was their way of showing their concern. For John it was like a homecoming.

They had no sooner finished their meal when the sound of a sleigh announced the return of the others. Everyone rushed outside to find the horses foaming and sweating from plowing through the deep snow. Jacques stood high on the seat of the sleigh, relieved that they had made it back to the camp. Beside him sat Meg, full of smiles, and in the back the other shantyman had wrapped Cameron warmly in blankets and was cradling him so that his leg would not feel the motion of the sleigh. In a moment they carried Meg and Cameron inside, while others led the team away to be rubbed down and stabled for the night.

The men crowded around Cameron. Carefully his trousers were eased over his broken leg, and his woollen underwear pushed up. Mrs. Ferguson crouched over and examined the leg. Around the middle of the shin bone the skin was swollen and tender. The cook examined the bone for a long time, running her finger and thumb up and down the bone until finally she was satisfied. It was a fracture, she announced to everyone, but it seemed to have set squarely back on the bone again. It would take a couple of weeks to heal, but it would be all right.

Mrs. Ferguson then supervised the making of the splints. Several strong pieces of birch that would stretch from Cameron's knee to his ankle were split away from a log. Then the cook took some strong cotton cloth, ripped it into long strips, and with the help of several other men she placed the splints carefully around the leg and wrapped the cotton around and around until it made a strong cast from the ankle to the knee to protect and strengthen the broken bone.

Once Meg and Cameron had something to eat and warmed themselves by the fire, they began feeling better. Both of them had slept fitfully while waiting to be picked up and now they felt relaxed and happy to be back in the shanty again.

Cameron explained what had happened on the trail. He seemed his old self again, joking gently with the others, a smile lurking at the corners of his mouth. As he came to the end of his story he gave credit to Meg and John. "You know if it wasn't for those two Bains kids I'd be out on the trail still. Let me tell you, Angus would be proud."

The two of them blushed deeply. To receive that type of recognition showed how much they had been accepted by the shantymen.

Not long afterwards Hardy and MacInnes barged into the shanty without warning. Hardy was huge and threatening; MacInnes tried to stand tall to make his tiny frame seem bigger. But in spite of efforts to impress they were somehow not as threatening as they had seemed in the past.

"The three of you will get out of my shanty!" Hardy said, indicating John, Meg and Cameron.

"Cameron's leg's broken. He can't walk," said one of the shantymen firmly.

"I don't care. I won't have them in my shanty!"

Without exception the men protested the order. "You can't do that, Hardy!" "You'll kill the man!" said another. "Putting an injured man on the trail is breaking the code of the shanties, Hardy!"

"I'm the foreman here!" Hardy shouted in return. "You men take orders from me!" But in some way his bellowed orders lacked their old ruthless forcefulness. He knew he was in a weak position.

The shantymen defied him openly. "If you force them out and they die, then you'll be held responsible, Hardy!" said Jacques.

"You're a murderer!" shouted another.

"Now look here!" said MacInnes anxiously. "Don't you men know your place? Mr. Hardy is your foreman, your leader, and you must follow him." MacInnes' haughty superiority made the men even angrier.

"These people are staying!" someone shouted. "And they'll get paid for it too. Didn't Cameron break his leg working for the company? He should get full wages until he's fit to work again."

"That's right," others agreed.

The mounting anger of the men stunned Hardy and MacInnes. They did not know what to say or do next. Meg felt a new excitement, and her impulsive nature pushed her into the argument. "You'd kill us all, just like you killed our father!" she shouted at Hardy. The foreman nearly cowered from the attack. "It's true isn't it?" Meg shouted, her finger pointing at him in a sharp stabbing motion. "You killed him because the union was getting too strong. Admit it!"

Hardy towered over the slim girl, but his strength seemed to drain from him in the face of the intensity of her attack. "No, I didn't," he said anxiously. "I didn't! Bains was killed by the tree."

Meg erupted again. "You killed him! Admit it! You killed him!" she shouted with such intensity that her voice was cracking.

The fear in Hardy's eyes said more than words. "I didn't do it! I didn't do it!" In sudden desperation, he opened the shanty door and fled into the night.

MacInnes was shocked by Hardy's flight. He tried to save something from the encounter. "The three of you will have to go," he said, but it was only a weak attempt to save face. Then he quickly followed Hardy out of the shanty.

CHAPTER 14

ANGRY scenes between Hardy and the shantymen had been enacted over and over since the beginning of the season, but now, for the first time, Hardy had been the one to back down. Sensing their new power, the men could hardly contain their impatience. Groups paced the floor of the small shanty talking loudly about what they would like to do to the foreman if they had the chance.

Gradually the anger subsided, and they sat around on the benches and bunks and talked about the day's events. It felt good for John and Meg to be back at home among the men, particularly since they seemed to have developed a new sense of unity and forcefulness. Just the morning before, when they had left, the men were faced with the defeat of their strike and the defeat of their union. Now they seemed stronger than ever, waiting impatiently for the next confrontation.

The talk quickly centred on the problems of the log chute. After John, Meg and Cameron had left the day before, Hardy had sent all of the men to work on the log chute. Everyone could see that it was vitally important to get it built before the spring run-off, or it would be impossible to get the timber downstream. If Percy did not get the timber to market he would not have enough money to pay his bills, his creditors would be onto him, and in a matter of months he would be bankrupt.

But the problem, as the men saw it, was that Hardy's plan for building the new chute was no different from the one that had collapsed a few days before. Instead of building the whole 150 yards of the chute from the ground up in one solid unit, he planned to build it from the top of the hill so that it protruded high up into the air with little support until the next section was built.

The horror of the collapse of the chute was still vivid in all of their minds, and many of the men nursed bruised muscles and broken ribs. The more they talked about it, the more they came to realize that Hardy's attempt to rebuild the chute in the same way as before was just another indication that he had no concern for their safety.

One of the older shantymen was particularly angry. "I tell you she'll collapse again, Cameron," he said in a loud voice so that everyone could hear. "Just as sure as I'm standing here, the first big blow and she'll come down like matchsticks and someone could be caught in it just like Tim."

"It's true," said one of the younger men. "But Hardy won't listen. It's like he thinks he knows everything and we know nothing. All he'll say is get back to work and stop complaining."

Cameron smiled. "The last strike didn't seem much of a success."

"We should just pack up and walk back home." said another. "They'll never get the chute finished in time, and they'll never get the timber down to Quebec City. That means Percy's company will be bankrupt before summer and most of us will never get paid for our season's work."

That was the first time that line of argument had occurred to any of the men, but the logic of it was compelling. It was well known that many lumber companies in the Ottawa Valley had gone bankrupt and their shantymen had never got paid for the season's work. To think that after months of isolation and hardship they might arrive home without a penny for their efforts was more than any of them could tolerate.

"We should pull out right away," one of the men said. "Let Hardy finish it," said another. "Serve him right. This company deserves to go bankrupt."

"But if it does go bankrupt then we all suffer," said Cameron. Many of us have families and it means we'd have no money to face the summer and fall. What about the work that we've already put in? All that would be lost."

The men talked about the issue for some time. Finally, Jacques spoke. "Hardy thinks that this way of building the chute is going to be faster and cheaper for him, but he doesn't realize that it'll take longer because it's bound to collapse again. If we started building it from the ground up, the way it should be built, it could be finished in time for the spring break-up. Do it his way and it'll never be done."

"We know that, but what'll we do?" said a shantyman with an edge of desperation in his voice.

The shanty was quiet. Everyone waited to hear what solution their leader could find. Cameron was deep in thought. His shoulders were hunched, his fingers lightly stroked his beard, and he stared steadily at the floor.

When he started talking he seemed very abstracted, as if he was still thinking through all the alternatives.

"We could leave the shanty and there's no question the Percy Lumber Company would be bankrupt before spring, but that way we'd run the risk of not getting our back wages. We could go on strike again and demand that Hardy change the way he's building the chute, but he used the guns on us the last time and he'd likely do it again. What we could do is just ignore him. That seems to be so simple, but it could work." Cameron was quiet for a moment, thinking through the strategy, and then he seemed to brighten in enthusiasm. "Jacques is right. Why don't we just go out tomorrow and begin to build the log chute the way we want to build it, and ignore Hardy, What could he do to us? We would all be working and the only thing is that we wouldn't take any orders from him. We'd build the chute the way we'd want to build it, not the way he wanted. That'd really make him angry, but what could he do? We're going to finish his log chute and finish it on time. The only difference is that we do it our way and not his."

The men were silent, trying to understand the implications of the new tactic. "What do you think, Jacques?" asked Cameron, seeking another opinion.

"I don't know," the other replied. "You're saying that we should just ignore Hardy like he wasn't there and build the chute the way we wanted."

"That's right."

"But he's the foreman," said one of the older shantymen, in a puzzled way. "How can we ignore him?"

"As long as we're working on the log chute what can he do? He can't force all of us at the same time to do what he wants, and anyway we'll finish the chute before spring break-up. It's just a way of telling him that we're going to do things our way from now on and not his way."

"That's the nice thing about it," said Jacques. "We get our own way because the chute's safe and still Hardy can't do anything to us."

Everyone smiled at the thought of how frustrated Hardy would be at learning he could do nothing to direct them. They talked about it in more detail, trying to anticipate Hardy's reaction. The more they discussed the plan, the more they liked it. Finally, they all agreed. The next morning they would let Hardy know that they would put up with him no longer. The men talked excitedly late into the night, developing strategies and counter-strategies in case anything went wrong. To a man they felt a new sense of optimism.

The next morning Meg and John were wakened long before dawn by Mrs. Ferguson, and they began their chores as if they had never been away. John stood shivering in the cold woodshed attached to the stable, and split firewood with the heavy broad axe. He filled up the wood boxes in both the camboose and foreman's shanties, and fetched water from the lake. Meg stayed inside, helping the cook prepare breakfast and the evening pot of pork and beans. They both worked as quickly as they could. They wanted to finish in time to go with the men to the log chute and witness the confrontation with Hardy.

By the time the shantymen were finished breakfast, Meg and John were ready to leave. As the men stood in the cold morning air, the expectation of the morning's events made everyone a little anxious. It was a crucial day for the union, and they knew they would have to show strength and determination or once again they could fail.

When they got to the log chute the men set to work immediately, tearing down what was left of the old trestle so they could start afresh. John and Meg cleared a space away, started a fire, and settled Cameron down beside it so that he could watch the proceedings. About half an hour after the work had begun, Hardy arrived.

He stood in the centre of a group of men, his hands on his hips, looking dismayed. "Here, what's this?" he said to no one in particular. "What's going on here?"

It was as if this was a signal, and all of the men downed their tools and converged on the foreman. For a moment Hardy seemed confused and near panic, seeing the men coming toward him, but he quickly collected himself and stood his ground, his hands on his hips, a defiant look on his face.

"What's going on here?" he repeated. An old shantyman was the first to answer. "We're building the chute our way, Hardy. We're not taking orders from you any more."

Hardy was still puzzled. "But why are you ripping it down?"

"We're starting all over again." said another. "Then we're going to rebuild it from the ground up so that it holds together in one piece. If we build it your way it'll collapse again and kill even more of us."

"I didn't tell you that you could do that!"

"We didn't ask you, Hardy. We're just going to do it. We don't care what you think. Your way is too dangerous. It'll collapse in the first big wind."

"You'll do it my way. I'm the foreman here!" Hardy shouted.

"We're not listening to you any more!" To a man they were grimly determined to win their point.

Hardy looked around desperately from man to man as if looking for someone who would give him support, but found none.

The foreman was at a loss. What could he do? The men were not on strike, and he could not force them back to work. In fact, they were promising to continue to work. The only thing they were doing was refusing to follow his plans to build the chute. What could he do? What could he say? Then he saw Cameron leaning up against a sleigh, quietly watching the argument, with Meg and John standing close beside him. Hardy's anger exploded.

"It's the three of you! This is your doing! Things were peaceful around here until you came back. You put the men up to this."

Cameron smiled. "Did it ever occur to you why the shantymen are rebelling against you, Hardy?"

But his attitude made the foreman even more furious. "I'll get you for this. All three of you will pay for it!"

The men moved in closer around the three union- ists as if to show their support. Jacques was close to Hardy and said, "If you try anything against those three you'll have to answer to all of us, Hardy!" It was a menacing threat, and it expressed the feelings of all of the men.

"And don't get your guns," he said. "If you try that again they may be turned against you."

The solid unity of the shantymen unnerved Hardy. In the past he had been able to intimidate them with his shouts and violence, but now they did not seem the least bit frightened. For almost a minute Hardy looked from man to man, his face reddening with anger, his mouth twitching uncontrollably.

Suddenly he could control his anger no longer. "I'll get you! Wait and see! I'll get you and you'll regret you ever signed on to come to my shanty!" He went back up the hill to his sleigh and with a crack of his whip he drove his team frantically back towards the camp.

CHAPTER 15

IN the next few weeks the men worked harder and accomplished more than they had since the beginning
of the season. It was already early March when they
started rebuilding the chute, and everyone knew that
spring break-up would be on them in a month. If they
did not get finished it was unlikely they would ever get
paid for their season's work, but even more important
than that, the men's pride was involved. They were determined to show Hardy that their way of building the
chute was the safest and in the long run the fastest way.

This new tactic of ignoring Hardy did more for the
morale of the men than anyone could have imagined.
Only a few days before, the men had merely gone
through the paces of their work as a routine, but now
everyone realized that each man had to contribute as
much as possible to their collective effort or they would
all fail. Their future depended on dedicated hard work,
and no one wanted to let his fellow shantymen down.

Hardy and MacInnes were furious, and tried as best
they could to sabotage the efforts of the men. Whenever
MacInnes had a chance to corner someone he would
threaten to juggle the books in such a way that the man
would lose pay if he did not co-operate. But it fell to
Hardy to carry on most of the work of undermining their
unity. He was constantly lurking around the log chute,

ordering the men around, telling them to do their jobs differently, but without exception they were strong in the face of the harassment and they simply ignored the two company men.

This was the most difficult of all things for Hardy to endure. Whether they hated him or not, the men had always been forced to listen to him in the past because he was the foreman and because he had the physical strength to impose his will, but now the men treated him as if he did not exist. He would pick out a shantyman and heap scorn on him, but rather than turning to fight and argue, each man in his turn just walked away and ignored everything that was said. As time went on, Hardy gradually grew silent, sulking around the work site, watching the men in the hope they would fail and the log chute would collapse.

But that was the impossibility of Hardy's position. On the one hand his impulse was to tear the men apart for daring to defy his word, but on the other he knew better than any other that if they did fail in completing the log chute they would all be finished. As soon as the company creditors heard the Percy Lumber Company was not going to get its winter cut out of the bush that season, they would call their loans and the company would be bankrupt within a week.

One night after supper, John was passing the foreman's shanty and overheard Hardy and MacInnes arguing. MacInnes was shouting uncontrollably in his thick Scottish burr. "Why don't you do something, Hardy? You're letting those low-born shantymen run all over you. Soon they'll be telling me what I'm to be doing!"

MacInnes went on for several minutes, ranting at Hardy as if he were a little child.

The next day Hardy again tried to reimpose his will. He arrived at the work site in the morning along with the men and began assigning them to different tasks as if he had always held control. But the men went about their work as if he were not there. Hardy began shouting uncontrollably at one of the younger shantymen who happened to be close by. Finally, he even pushed the man, trying to promote a fight. Suddenly, fifteen angry shantymen simultaneously downed their tools and surrounded the raving foreman. They said nothing, but their actions left no doubt about the message. They would put up with this type of bullying no longer.

Hardy stopped in mid-sentence. For a moment he was defiant, but the solidarity of the group gave him a sudden fright. He retreated, shaken and defeated, to lurk once again around the edges of the work site.

But even though Hardy had been decisively defeated and the morale of the men was high, the work progressed very slowly. The log chute had to run 150 yards from the edge of Cache Lake down to the quiet waters of the Madawaska River below the waterfall. At first the land fell away gradually and the trestle did not have to be built high above the ground, but there was a sharp, almost vertical, drop and the log chute had to be built fifty and sixty feet above the ground for a distance of over a hundred yards. This was the most difficult part to build, and it was here that it had collapsed in the storm.

The men's agreement to work from the bottom up, building the trestle as one strong, solid unit, made the job far more difficult. Before, they had been able to use a horse and rope and slide the heavy log struts down the completed part of the chute and slowly lower them into place. Now, to get the struts positioned they had to be winched into the air using a rig of a huge tripod mounted next to the chute. A rope went from the log strut lying on the ground through a pulley on top of the tripod and over to a team of horses. With a signal from the men on top of the chute, the teamster would start his horses and the log would be slowly pulled to the top of the tripod. When it was within reach, the men on the chute, holding on by wrapping their legs around some support, would grab the log with their hands, or with long pikes, and wrestle it into place. All the time the teamster had to work his horses with delicate skill. He would back them up to give the slack to lower the log into place, then take them forward a little to raise it, then back again until the log fitted perfectly. All the time the men shouted instructions. "Give me a little more!" "Hold her too!" "Up a touch!" Finally, the log would be worked into the exact position and the hammers would ring out, driving the long steel pins to hold the struts in place.

Altogether there were three crews of men positioned along the length of the log chute involved in the actual building of the trestle. Two men on the ground looked after the horses and selected the struts, and another four men up on the chute planned and executed the task of placing them. Other men worked in pairs in the bush, finding and cutting good solid timbers of about a foot in thickness for use in the chute. After it was cut, the log would be snaked out of the bush with a single horse and left in a pile to be dressed for use in the trestle. The hewers, the most expert axemen in the camp, then used their broad axes to shave the ends into wedges or squares, and cut them to length according to need.

The different jobs took a tough physical toll on the men, but they still kept in good spirits. Because there was no foreman each man was self-motivated and self-directed; with little effort they welded themselves into smoothly functioning units. They all grew to know the strengths and limits of the others, and each man was able to find a level where he could contribute the most to the overall effort.

John and Meg threw themselves into their work with as much enthusiasm as the others. At the first call of Mrs. Ferguson in the morning they got up, dressed without a word and began their chores. By now they could work with ease. One would go out of doors to haul in the water, help the teamsters and carry and split firewood, while the other helped the cook prepare the meals.

At first John insisted that because he was the oldest and a boy he should do all the outside work, but his sister would have none of that.

"Who do you think you are, John Bains?" Meg said angrily. "Why should I get stuck inside all the time?"

"You're a girl and that's the type of work you should do."

"I will not," Meg said, stamping her foot. "I can do the outside work just as easily as you. I can split wood just as fast, and harness a horse just as well. It's not fair!"

"But I thought you'd want to work in the shanty," John said defensively.

"No! I want to do all the jobs just like you."

"All right, all right, we'll share the work equally."

True to his word, from that time on John and Meg shared all the work. One morning John would do the outside chores and the next Meg would take her turn. The boy knew that if he did not give in there was no way he would have a moment's peace for the rest of the season.

Every day by mid-morning the two finished their shanty chores, packed up the lunch for the men and headed for the log chute. Once they got there they took turns preparing the lunch or pitching in to help the men. Within the next few weeks they gained more and more experience. Often Meg would find herself up in the skeleton of the trestle wrestling a log strut into place, and frequently someone would turn a horse over to John and he would spend the afternoon snaking logs out of the bush. It was hard work for everyone, but it was especially satisfying to John and Meg because it was their chance to begin to learn the work of the shantymen. They were becoming accepted as equals by the others and that was very important to them.

Of all the worries of the shantymen, the one that concerned them the most was the weather. They had been working on their plan for no more than a week when the temperature soared well above freezing. The snow melted and water poured off the hills in small rivulets, collecting in deep puddles. The ice on the lake cracked with loud booming noises that sounded like the rumbling of artillery in the distance. Everyone knew that if the warm spell lasted it would be only a matter of days till the ice would be too soft to walk on, and then overnight the spring break-up would be on them. If that happened the log chute would never be finished in time to catch the spring run-off. That day everyone worked frantically, as if trying to complete it in a rush, but the next day the temperature dropped and everything refroze solidly.

Still they were working against time. By the end of March everyone knew that each extra day it took to finish was pushing their luck. They all worked incessantly from dawn to well after dark, and the trestle slowly grew higher and higher over the ground they had to traverse, but the higher it grew the longer the tripods had to be, and the more dangerous it was for the men perched high up in the skeleton of the trestle. The work seemed to go so slowly that the progress seemed imperceptible and yet, finally, all the struts were in place. The hewers had planed the planks that were to sit on the top of the chute and let the water flush the big squared timbers down its run, and then, finally, they even had those in place. All that was left was the last twenty-five yards of trestle, and that was so low it needed little bracing.

The very day the men finished the most difficult part of the log chute, Percy arrived by cutter from Ottawa.

CHAPTER 16

MacINNES was in the foreman's shanty working on the books when the sleigh arrived. When he noticed it was the company owner, Mr. Percy, he rushed outside and began acting as if nobility had arrived. Meg was in the camp at the time, fetching materials from the store-house, and she watched the proceedings from behind the shed. The shanty clerk bowed a number of times out of respect for his superior, offering his hand as assistance in getting out of the cutter and nervously repeating over and over again how nice it was to see him, what an honour it was for the men in the camp to have him visit, and how welcome everyone would make him feel.

Percy listened with an attitude of superiority to the flattering remarks that MacInnes showered on him. He was dressed as a wealthy man even in this wild place: his black merino wool coat shone in its brilliance, he wore soft doeskin gloves and fine knee-length leather boots, his white wing-collared shirt sported a grey conservative ascot tie with a pearl stickpin and on top of his head perched a round bowler hat that might have been fashionable with the wealthy businessmen of Ottawa but looked comically out of place in the harsh, isolated forests of Algonquin Highlands. He was the picture of the prosperous Ottawa timber merchant: soft and weak with sagging jowls and protruding stomach. What an incredible contrast, Meg thought, between this soft city merchant and the hard, lean, windburned shantymen who worked for him. Percy would not survive a day's work, and yet he owned everything and had the power to control every man in the camp.

It was only after MacInnes had ushered Percy ceremoniously into the foreman's shanty that Meg recognized that his chauffeur was O'Riley. It had been a long time since anyone from the outside world had come into the shanty, and it was particularly good to see the teamster whom they had grown so close to on their trip up the Opeongo Line. Meg hugged him warmly and began recounting all the things that had happened to them since their arrival. After blanketing and feeding the animals, she took the teamster down to the log chute to announce Percy's arrival.

The shantymen were bitter when they learned of the news. It foretold changes that could easily get beyond their control. Within a matter of hours this proved to be true. Hardy went from sulking on the outskirts of the work site to arrogantly ordering the men around whenever Percy was present. The men complained bitterly under their breath, but they followed the orders because they were reluctant to show Percy what had happened in the shanty until they were able to get some idea of what response this would lead to. Fortunately for both sides, a confrontation was avoided because Hardy, MacInnes and Percy spent so much time locked in the forman's shanty that they had little time to be with the men.

The two foremen catered to Percy's every desire. A special bunk was made for him in the foreman's shanty, Mrs. Ferguson was assigned to sew up a mattress stuffed with fresh hay, and she was ordered to cover it with the best blankets in the camp. Special meals of venison and beef were prepared for the company men while the shantymen kept with the monotonous diets of beans, salt pork, bread and tea. Everyone grumbled in dissatisfaction, but did nothing but wait and watch.

The day after he arrived, Percy came out to the log chute for a tour directed by Hardy and MacInnes. The men were gathered around an open fire eating a lunch of half-frozen pork and blackstrap, and sipping strong cups of tea. MacInnes rushed ahead of Percy to carefully place a heavy buffalo robe neatly over a log so the company president could sit beside the men but not get his clothes wet from the snow.

Percy's fat, expensively dressed figure contrasted with the rough mackinaw coats and course woollen workpants of the shantymen. He put on an air of confidence by talking in a friendly way, but the men continued eating their lunch without a word. They could sense that Percy's friendship was just a show to lure them into thinking he was one of them. "You men have worked hard this season," he said with a smile.

The men continued eating silently without any indication that they had heard him. Percy tried again. "You've done a good job on that log chute. I must say it's a capital job."

Again there was no answer. Percy looked for a friendly face among the forty men circling the fire, but they all avoided his eyes. He turned to Hardy. "You must have had to work the men hard, Mr. Hardy, to get this chute finished on time."

A restlessness stirred through the men. The comment made it obvious that Hardy had not told Percy about the dispute over the building of the chute. Hardy gave a faint smile and nod as if in appreciation of the compliment, but all the time he eyed the men warily.

Percy tried again to engage the men in conversation. "Looks like a good chute to me. Good and solid."

One of the men, sitting on the far side of the fire, finally spoke. He looked at the ground so that the company men would not recognize him, but loud enough for everyone to hear. "It's no thanks to Hardy."

"What's that?" said Percy.

"We should go now, Mr. Percy," said Hardy. He realized the scene could suddenly become ugly.

"What did that man mean?" said Percy, angry that he was being ignored.

Hardy was on his feet. "Let's go up and look at the timber now, sir. I'll explain it later." He wanted to get Percy as far away from the men as possible before they began showing their real anger and resentment.

Percy scowled and guffawed pompously, as if trying to show that he was insulted that the men had not taken up his gesture of friendship, but he let himself be led away to the cutter and the three of them sped back to the safety of the shanty.

The men quietly went on sipping their tea and staring blankly into the fire as if nothing had happened, but each of them turned the same thoughts over in his mind. They had toiled all season under the harsh demands set by Hardy; they had faced danger, isolation and loneliness, but for what? So that Percy, that fat, vain man who understood little about their hardships and cared even less, could make a huge profit.

The enormity of it all sickened John. Their father had been killed, Tim was dead, the whole way of life of their family, and of others like it, had been disrupted, and for what? So a bigger profit could be made for Percy. He was solidly committed to the union now, and had to see it through to the end. "What are we going to do?" he said loud enough for everyone to hear. "We've built them a long chute. Maybe we did it our own way, but it hasn't done us any good. Now that it's built they'll be able to float the timber down the Madawaska and Percy's going to make another huge profit for himself, but where does that leave us? We take all the risks and he makes all the profits."

Many of the men shifted uncomfortably but they were silent. "What are we going to do?" John asked again bitterly. "Hardy's killed two of us this season and we've done nothing. They'll pay us off in Ottawa or Quebec City and that'll be the end of it." John's bitterness gave him a sense of strength.

"We should go on strike again," said Meg defiantly.

"We'd just get smashed again." said another.

"Why do we care? Let's just go out on strike and stay out so long that they miss the spring runoff and we ruin the company," came the bitter reply from one of the young men.

"But if we did strike we could limit ourselves to the issue of getting the union recognized." said Jacques. "That'd be at least something we could try and achieve. What do you think, Cameron?"

Cameron was quiet, pondering the situation before speaking. "Remember that we lost the last strike because no one would stay out and fight. How do we know it won't happen again?"

But things had changed considerably since the last strike. The season was almost at an end, and within two or three weeks the ice would be off the lake. In order to get ready for the log drive the preparations had to be speeded up or they would make a late start. Percy's arrival meant they could deal directly with him rather than Hardy. But, more important than anything else, the last few weeks had shown that the company could be defeated. No longer was Hardy the frightening, overpowering figure who could use his physical strength to intimidate them; he was as weak and vulnerable as anyone else.

All the shantymen could clearly see that the situation was different. "There's real unity among us now, Cameron," John argued. "We're strong and the company is in a weak position." The men agreed enthusiastically.

They discussed the pros and cons of a strike as realistically as possible for half an hour or more, and at every stage they agreed that if the time was ever ripe it was now. Still Cameron was not completely satisfied. "I think we should have a show of hands to see who's in favour of having a strike and who's opposed. That way we can clearly see how everyone thinks." The men agreed. "All in favour of a strike," Cameron asked. A forest of hands went up. "All opposed." No one moved.

After the vote the men cheered and laughed happily. There was a sense of excitement and expectation, for again they were launched on a strike that could make or break them all.

Jacques held his hands in the air for silence. "During the last strike we had no leader. This time we should have someone to act as our spokesman and talk to Percy on our behalf. I say we should elect Cameron for he is the strongest among us. He is the one who has fought long and hard for the union and he is the one we all respect." The others agreed, but again Jacques insisted that they hold a vote. It was another unanimous decision, and Cameron was now the official leader of the men.

Cameron leaned against the sleigh, stroking his beard, thinking of what the strike would bring. He was quiet for almost a minute and then he held up his hands for silence. "I will be your spokesman," he said. "I am honoured to play that role, but remember I have been only one of many in this camp that has fought for a union. It started with Angus Bains a long time ago, and with his leadership the idea of a union has grown until now it includes every shantyman in the camp. Remember as well that I am only your spokesman. You are the ones who make the decisions in this union. A leader is only as strong as those who follow. The company will try to divide us and set one against the other. We can defeat them only with our solidarity. Together we can win, but if each stands alone we are all lost."

The union was new, with unfamiliar tactics and different goals, but every man in the camp from the sophisticated hewer to the lowly cook's help could understand its principle. As long as the workers had the unity of purpose to act together, it did not matter what the wealth and power of the company, it would ultimately have to listen seriously to what they had to say.

The discussion of tactics went on for another hour. Some men thought they should go back and occupy the camboose shanty and refuse to move until they had won their demands. Others thought Hardy would automatically force them out, arguing again that the shanty was private property. Finally, it was agreed that they would take supplies from the company and camp overnight in the hills around the log chute. Meg, John and O'Riley, the teamster, were chosen to go back to the camp for the supplies because it was felt that they would arouse the least suspicion among the company men.

When they arrived back at the shanty, with a large open sleigh pulled by two big Clydesdales, John went to find the cook. Mrs. Ferguson welcomed the plan and left what she was doing to help load the sleigh. "Let's hurry," she warned. "All the company men are away but they could come back at any moment."

They manoeuvred the big sleigh in behind the storage shed that was attached to the stables, opened the doors wide and began the loading. They were half finished when Meg thought she heard something. She cautiously looked around the end of the shed. Hardy, MacInnes and Percy were heading back across the frozen lake in their cutter.

"They're almost here!" she whispered to the others.

"Let's hurry!" said O'Riley anxiously.

The door of the shed opened away from the camp so that it concealed them from the company men. The four of them worked furiously, loading two full hogsheads of pork, a sack of beans and two bags of flour aboard the sleigh.

"Let's go!" O'Riley whispered.

"No!" said John "We need the canvas to make the tents!"

"We don't have time!"

"They're high up in the rafters." said Mrs. Ferguson.

Meg and John scrambled up. "Hurry!" whispered O'Riley. "I can hear them coming."

They tore at the canvas, the rough material burning their hands. Their arms and backs were aching with the effort, but gradually they wrestled the heavy pieces of material free and they flopped to the ground and the others loaded them onto the sleigh. Sheet after sheet they tossed down, until finally the loft was empty.

Just as they were finishing they heard Percy's cutter coming into camp. The voices of the three company men could be heard as they stood in front of the shanties talking.

"Let's spread a canvas over the whole load," whispered Mrs. Ferguson. "Then they won't be able to see what's in the sleigh." Quickly they unfolded a heavy sheet, spread it over the load and tied it securely at the four corners.

They were still not out of trouble. Each of them tried to catch their breath. "How do we get past Hardy?" whispered John.

"We'll have to bluff our way past," replied O'Riley.

"But what if he finds out?"

"We'll have to take that chance."

"That's all you can do," whispered Mrs. Ferguson. "I'll see you down at the log chute as soon as I get my gear." She disappeared towards the camboose shanty.

"Let's go out as easily as we're able." said O'Riley with his hands on the shoulders of both John and Meg. "If we act suspicious Hardy's bound to stop us."

The three of them climbed up onto the rig. O'Riley picked up the reins, eased the heavily loaded sleigh around the edge of the shed and down between the buildings of the camp towards the ice-covered lake. They were moving past the foreman's shanty when Hardy called out. "Hey there, O'Riley. Pull up here. What have you got in that load?"

O'Riley had no choice but to rein in his horses. Hardy walked quickly over from the doorway of the foreman's shanty. He was gruff and serious. "Heavy load you've got."

O'Riley tried to be casual but still convincing. "It's just some supplies that the men need."

Hardy walked around the back of the sleigh, vaguely inspecting the load as if he felt something was wrong but could not pinpoint the trouble. It was tense. Each of them thought that at any moment he would untie a corner rope, throw back the canvas, and see what they were carrying.

John felt he had to say something to divert Hardy's attention, "Nice to have Mr. Percy in camp, sir."

"Eh?" said Hardy in surprise. "Oh yes, that it is. He's a good boss, too. Isn't he boy?"

"Yes sir. That's true."

"You let the other men know that he's the best boss of all the shanties," Hardy said gruffly. His attention seemed to be distracted from the contents of the load and to the bigger issue of the morale of the men.

"Yes sir, I certainly will, sir," John said cheerfully. "Goodbye now, Mr. Hardy." John knew that his friendliness was forced, but Hardy did not seem to notice. O'Riley flicked the reins and the sleigh set out again. John looked back to see Hardy still watching them, then he turned and disappeared into the foreman's shanty.

The men were still working when they got back to the log chute. A small crew had scouted around and chosen a campsite high up on a hill, giving a good view of the chute and out onto Cache Lake. O'Riley expertly guided the horses up a narrow trail to the site and they quickly unloaded the sleigh.

When they finished, John and Meg went to where the men were working and found Cameron. "It's done," Meg said. "We've got the supplies."

Cameron's face broke into a broad smile that crinkled his eyes. He put a hand on each of their shoulders. "Have any trouble?"

John smiled in return. "We managed."

Already the men were converging around them. Cameron's face brightened, and he climbed up onto a pile of logs so everyone could see and hear him. "Men!" he shouted. Everyone listened expectantly, "Men, we have the food and supplies. Let's down tools. We're on strike!"

Whistles and shouts came from the circling men; those still some distance away heard the shouts, knew what it was, and joined in the chorus. All over the work site the men were downing their tools and unharnessing the animals. It was the beginning of the strike.

As a group the men climbed up the hill to prepare the camp site. They worked for another hour in a laughing, jovial mood. Some took shovels and snowshoes to scrape away the loose snow, others went out to cut firewood and haul it back to the site. Another group cut hemlock boughs to make mattresses and still others rigged the canvas on poles to make tents. They worked easily, enjoying the change of pace. There was no rush; they had the rest of the day to make preparations.

It was near sunset when one of the men came running up the slope shouting. "Cameron! Cameron! It's Hardy and the others. They're coming back!"

Excitement swept through the men. As a group they came decisively down the hill to meet the company men, each man wearing a look of determination. Quickly they circled the cutter that had just drawn up. Hardy, Percy and MacInnes sat in it wondering what had happened. "What's going on here?" Hardy asked in disbelief.

Cameron stood a step or two in front of the others. "We're on strike, Hardy," he said in a calm, even voice that betrayed no emotion.

"On strike? Why? I don't understand."

Cameron replied coolly. "We've decided we won't work any more until we get our demands."

Hardy was suddenly his old angry self again. His face was flushed, his scar a violent red. "I'll not have that. You men get back to work right now or you'll be sorry you ever thought of a strike!"

"No one's going back, Hardy. We've all agreed. Either we get our demands or we go back down the

Opeongo Line and leave you to do the log drive yourself!"

Cameron kept calm. "And from now on we deal with Percy." He looked at the company owner. "These are our demands, so listen to them carefully. There are only two: firstly, we want Hardy and MacInnes fired. We won't work for them again. And second, we want our union recognized so that we can negotiate directly with you. Give us these two demands, Mr. Percy, and we will go back to work immediately."

Percy seemed confused. "I don't understand the meaning of all of this. We need you men to work or how will we get the logs down to the Ottawa River?" His shock indicated that he was ignorant of the bitter disputes that had been going on in the shanty since the beginning of the season.

"We're on strike, Percy!" One of the men shouted from the other side of the crowd. "We're not doing anything until we get our demands!"

Percy plucked himself up to his full height, trying to give the impression of importance. "But, you can't do that. It's illegal. We won't let you!"

"We don't care what your law says about strikes, Percy," said another. "We're not finished that log chute and we're not working on the log run until we get our demands!"

For the first time Percy seemed to understand the seriousness of the situation. "But ... but, if you do that, then I can't sell my logs and I'll go bankrupt!"

"That's right," said Cameron. "Maybe now that you understand you'll begin to listen to us."

Hardy had been silent, glaring at the men, his face red with anger, his eyes narrowing almost to slits. Suddenly, he pointed a finger at Cameron and shouted. "I'll get you! You wait and see! I'll make you pay for this, Cameron!" Without warning he hit the team of horses with the reins. They lurched and then started into a wild gallop. Men scurried to get out of their way. Hardy veered the frightened animals in a circle and then drove them hard up the hill. The men could see Percy looking wildly around as if still trying to understand this new and strange situation.

CHAPTER 17

THE next morning was a beautiful spring day. Warm southern breezes had reached deep into the Algonquin Highlands and a clear sky let the late March sun bake the land. The snow was melting so quickly that creeks were created everywhere; the trees dripped and puddles collected in every hollow. Overnight it was the beginning of a new season and the end of the old.

Meg and John had slept together under canvas on beds of hemlock boughs. John woke with a start when he felt the cold melted snow washing up against his legs, and when he rolled over he woke his sister. For a moment the strange place disoriented them, but then they remembered the strike. Hurriedly they scrambled out of bed, dressed, rolled up their blankets and went outside.

It was late. Already the sun was high in the sky and the camp was mostly deserted. Meg spotted Mrs. Ferguson bending over a fire and the two of them rushed over full of apologies for oversleeping. The cook only smiled. "We thought we'd let you sleep in. I had plenty of hands to help me this morning."

The two helped themselves to heaping platefuls of Mrs. Ferguson's special preparation of beans, pork and blackstrap, took big chunks of fresh baked bread, filled their cups with hot black tea that was bubbling over the fire and went to join a group of shantymen sunning themselves on some rocks. The contrast between this strike and the one they had been through a month before was obvious. Not only was the weather so warm that they could sit outside in their shirtsleeves, but they were much better prepared, and, most important, the morale was high.

John and Meg listened to the men chat as they ate their breakfast. They seemed ready for anything. Victory would not be easy, and in fact they talked openly of the possibility of having to desert the camp, but there was a sense of quiet determination about them all. They were determined either to win a final victory or face the collapse of everything they had worked for all season. There seemed to be no middle ground.

After breakfast the two cook's help washed their plates and cups in a tub of soapy water by the fire and went in search of Cameron. It took some looking, but finally they found him sitting alone on a hill overlooking the lake, watching the quiet scene as if the strike was the last thing on his mind.

After a few words of welcome Meg and John settled beside the shantyman and for some time they watched in silence. The lake was rapidly changing. The snow on the ice was melting fast, leaving huge, growing puddles. The sound of explosions came to them periodically, marking the break-up of the ice. It was still safe to carry a sleigh, but it would not be for long. Soon the ice would break up in huge ice floes which would slowly begin moving with the current towards the river. A few days more of warm weather and even the ice floes would break up. By then the rivers would be in full spring flood and the log drive would have to begin, to make sure that the huge square timbers would have enough water to get flushed down the narrow river of the Upper Madawaska.

The mild weather would bring a new life in the bush. Trees and plants would send out new shoots and the undergrowth would become thick and tangled. The hibernating animals would come back out again, and those who had spent the winter foraging for food would find the times easier. For almost a month the snowy owl that had patrolled the lake had gone north to the arctic, and soon the thousands of species of birds would return from the south.

The quiet was so absorbing that when Cameron started to talk it was a surprise to both Meg and John. "This is a strange country. One day it's frozen hard, and the next the snow melts into rivers. One day we're cutting and dressing timber, and the next we're rushing to complete the log chute. In three weeks' time, all going well, we'll be on the log drive."

Cameron was quiet for a moment and then began again. "The two of you have changed over this season. Do you remember, John, when you first got to this shanty you couldn't make up your mind on the union? Now you're both among the strongest supporters in the shanty. Your father, Angus, would be proud of both of you."

Cameron was a changed man too. Since their return from their trip in the bush, Cameron's leg had completely healed and he had developed into a resourceful leader of the union. He was not looking forward to the confrontation with the company men, but when it came he was ready.

They sat for a while longer, quietly chatting about the season's work but soon they got restless from the inactivity and went back down the hill to see what was happening around the camp. Little had changed. The shantymen seemed to be treating the strike as if it were a Sunday. Some spent time sharpening their knives and axes on whetstones, others went into the bush to haul firewood, and a large group congregated around the pool at the bottom of the waterfall with fishing lines, casting for bass and brook trout.

The men seemed totally relaxed, but both Meg and John could not get rid of the idea that they were on strike. It was as if they expected that at any moment there could be a violent eruption, and yet still nothing happened. They sat together by the waterfall sharing their anxieties. Why didn't the company men come? What were they plotting? On the surface the camp seemed peaceful, almost contented, but underneath there was a life-and-death struggle that could not be resolved without a bitter confrontation.

Lunch came, and for a time afterwards the men sat in the sun laughing and joking. When they finally broke up numbers of them lounged around chatting or half-heartedly doing chores. John and Meg found themselves moving around restlessly. They were both more and more anxious about the impending confrontation, and felt compelled to do something about it. Finally, the two of them climbed the hill that overlooked the lake and watched for the arrival of the company men.

Occasionally they would talk, but avoided any mention of the strike. It was as if each knew exactly what the other was thinking and there was no point in talking about it. Finally, late in the afternoon, John thought he saw a sleigh out on the ice coming towards them. They both stood up and strained to see. After a minute there was no mistaking it. Hardy was driving the cutter through pools of water on the ice. Beside him, still dressed like the Ottawa gentleman, sat Percy, and behind them on the small perch of the cutter crouched MacInnes.

Meg and John ran down into the camp and spread out in different directions, shouting at the top of their lungs. "They're coming! They're coming!" Immediately other runners spread out to collect the dispersed shantymen, and quickly everyone collected at the top of the log chute beside Cache Lake.

No sooner had they gathered than the cutter rounded the point of land and came into view. Percy's pair of high-spirited black Arabian horses were running at a full gallop, kicking up showers of water from their hooves and the runners of the cutter. Hardy drove wildly, without slowing until the cutter reached the shore about twenty yards away from the men; then he reined in so violently that even this pair of well-trained animals reared back in terror.

Hardy's anger was consuming him. He was bareheaded and his thick shock of brown hair flowed wildly backwards in the wind. Once the horses had calmed themselves he unfolded his huge frame out of the cutter, reached back inside for his Winchester, and turned on the shantymen. He looked determined to stop the strike at any price.

MacInnes, half Hardy's size, scrambled out of the back of the cutter and came out wielding the heavy shotgun. He, too, had a determined look about him. Percy followed behind, emptyhanded, shielding himself behind the two others.

Hardy's mouth twitched as he fought to control his anger. He had been ignored for over a month, and forced to suppress his hostility. Now was his chance for revenge. He shouted wildly at the shantymen. "What you do is illegal! You all know that! I warn you, I want this strike to stop now or there's no telling what might happen!" His voice was menacing. There was no doubt that Hardy was perfectly capable of using the weapons on anyone who stood in his way.

"Put those guns down, Hardy, before someone gets hurt!" Cameron demanded.

"No one's talking to you, Cameron!"

"If you use those guns you'll live to regret it."

"You shut up, Cameron, or I'll blow you off the face of the earth!" Hardy lifted the Winchester to his shoulder and pointed it straight at Cameron's chest.

"I'll not be quiet. I'm the spokesman for these men!"

"Either you be quiet or I'll silence you!"

Meg was standing with the others. Another word and it looked as if Hardy's gun would erupt, killing Cameron on the spot. She felt compelled to stop it at any price. Impulsively she stepped in front of Cameron to act as a shield.

"Get away!" Hardy shouted. But Meg came a step closer. "Get back or you'll get shot!" But she came still closer. "I'll do it. I'll kill you!" Hardy was desperate. What could he do? If he killed the girl it would set the men on a rampage which would not stop until they had destroyed everything. What hope would he have against forty shantymen? How could he deal with this girl? He was desperate.

Meg came towards him a step at a time, without a word. "Keep back!" Hardy shouted again, and he backed up a pace. "Keep back or I'll shoot!" But Meg had broken his nerve. The girl was directly in front of him now and she gently pushed the barrel of the gun harmlessly aside. Taking it out of his hands, she swiftly ejected the cartridges onto the ground. Then, going over to MacInnes, she calmly took the shotgun out of his hands, broke it open and removed the two shells. Methodically she walked over to the cutter, placed the weapons inside and returned to Cameron's side.

"Have you come to talk about our demands?" Cameron asked as if nothing had happened.

This angered Hardy even more. "No!" he shouted. "We've come to tell you to get back to work! It's against the law to strike!"

"You should know that isn't going to make any difference to us," said Cameron calmly. "We have all decided that if we don't win then the three of you can take these logs down the Madawaska yourself, because we're not going on the drive with you. It's up to Percy. If he doesn't agree to our demands then we'll all just walk back down the Opeongo Line and read about the bankruptcy of the Percy Lumber Company in the newspapers."

"Now see here," Percy replied pompously. "This doesn't seem right to me. I pay you men to work for me and I want you to go back to work and that's all there is to it."

"Do you know what it's been like working in this camp, Percy? Did you know about Tim's death? Do you really know how Bains died? What do you think caused those deaths?"

"They were accidents, both of them accidents."

Cameron spoke calmly and slowly so that Percy could hear every word that he was saying. "They were no accidents, Percy. At best they were caused by neglect. Remember that, because it's on your conscience too. We've had to put up with Hardy's ruthlessness all season, and we'll put up with it no longer. That's why we want our union. Let me just go over our demands in case you've forgotten them. We want Hardy and MacInnes fired, never to work for you again, and we want our union recognized and a promise that you'll always deal with us directly. Our demands are simple, Percy, but we're not going to back down until we get them, remember that. We're not working again until they're met!"

"You're not getting anything!" Hardy shouted frantically. He had been pacing back and forth, clenching and unclenching his fists as if barely able to contain himself. "Let me tell you shantymen that Percy and I have decided that if you won't go back to work we'll get the police to force you back. What you do is against the law, and we're going to see that the law is enforced. That means the police are going to come and put you all in jail, and if the police won't come then the army will come. I want you men back at work!" he shouted. "Do you understand?"

Cameron laughed scornfully, "You don't really think that we are that stupid, Hardy. Do you really think that the police will come all the way from Renfrew? Even if they came, by the time they got here they'd be too late to do anything. We'd have all walked back down the Opeongo Line, and there'd be no way of getting the timber out this season. Percy has to negotiate with us, so don't use idle threats that you can't deliver."

"Shut up, Cameron!" Hardy shouted.

"We've won this time, Hardy, and you know it. You're not our dictator any more."

Hardy had moved forward. He stood tall and threatening, his huge figure looming menacingly over Cameron. "You just shut up!" he shouted.

"This time you're finished, Hardy! Get that through your head. Your time in this shanty is over!"

Hardy made a motion to go for him. "I'll kill you for that, Cameron!"

"Yes, just the way you killed Angus Bains and Tim!"

"I didn't kill anyone!" Hardy's face was contorted. His fists were doubled, ready to strike.

"I know you did! You killed Bains and then you put him under the tree for us to find him. Every man in the shanty knows that!"

"Shut up! Damn it!" Hardy shouted uncontrollably. "I won't have you say it."

"You won't have me say the truth!"

"Shut up or I'll kill you too!" Hardy's anger consumed him. He pounced, his right fist exploding across Cameron's jaw, catching him with such force that the shantyman reeled backwards dazed and disoriented. Hardy pressed his advantage by following with a left and then a roundhouse right that knocked Cameron to the ground.

Hardy had completely lost control. He was on top of Cameron, pressing his knees into his chest and groin with his full weight. He was going to kill him; beat him to death with his fists. John had to do something. In an impulse the boy rushed Hardy from behind and struck him so hard he knocked him flying.

Cameron staggered to his feet, groggy and disoriented, but determined to see the fight to the end.

Hardy attacked again, but Cameron was able to slip away. The big man became so angered he rose up to an enormous height, his arms over his head like a bear.

Cameron retreated and found himself on the spillway of the log chute. He was trapped with Hardy blocking the only exit. He had no altenative but to move backwards with Hardy pursuing his every step.

Hardy rushed him, swinging his fist with such violence that when he missed it seemed as if he might lose his balance and pitch over the side. He pursued Cameron further and further out onto the log chute so that the two men were at its highest point, sixty feet above the bare rocks. Hardy's madness was complete. He was consumed with a passion to finish Cameron once and for all.

In a sudden lunge Hardy caught him and the two men went down onto the spillway of the chute, wrestling sixty feet above the rocks. Cameron had an arm free and he was pounding Hardy with all his strength, but the big man shrugged off the blows as if they were nothing. With a shout he swung his massive fist and caught Cameron full in the face. He swung again and

Cameron's body jerked into semi-consciousness. Hardy was on top of him, his huge hands around his throat, holding him far out over the edge of the trestle above the jagged rocks, choking the life out of him.

John was onto the chute. He had to save Cameron's life. Hardy was still choking the inert body when the boy reached them. He pounded on Hardy's back, then tried to pull him off, but he could not budge the huge weight. He struck him hard, then pushed against him with all his might. Hardy turned his head as if snapping out of a dream. The boy saw the complete madness in his eyes; he had lost all control.

Hardy dropped Cameron and with one sweep of his enormous arm knocked John onto the deck of the log chute. He stood his full height above the boy, his arms in the air. He would kill him. He let out an enormous roar and suddenly dove on top of John with the full weight of his body. The boy buckled his legs to protect himself. He caught Hardy in the pit of his stomach. He heaved the massive weight with all the strength in his legs. Hardy's body pitched up and then slipped over the edge of the log chute. John caught a glimpse of his suddenly startled face. Hardy made a desperate grab at the edge of the chute, but missed, and then disappeared over the side of the chute. A piercing shriek of terror filled the air, then a dull thump, then silence.

John lay on his back, stunned. He shook himself and looked over the side of the trestle. There on the rocks below lay the crumpled body of the big man. For a long time he stared at the dark unmoving heap. Thoughts streamed through his mind of his father, and of Tim and the whole scene of the shanty.

"John! John! Are you all right?" Meg shouted, tears streaming down her face. For a moment he could say nothing. He just continued to stare at the crumpled body on the rocks below, trying to understand what it all meant. "Are you all right?" Meg pleaded for an answer, cradling her brother's head in her hands.

"Is Hardy dead?" John stammered.

"Yes, he's dead."

"And Cameron?"

There were other men trying to relieve Cameron. His face was bloodied and swollen, but he stirred. "He's alive!" someone shouted. "Cameron's alive!" the word was shouted from man to man.

CHAPTER 18

JOHN and Meg viewed the crumpled remains of Hardy in horror when the body was brought up from the rocks. Why did it have to come to this? What was their responsibility? John, still in a state of shock, started to cry uncontrollably, and Meg joined him.

Each of the shantymen came in turn to console them. They repeated in many different ways that no one could be held responsible for Hardy's death. Hardy had even admitted murdering their father. He would certainly have killed Cameron if John had not intervened. Gradually the two of them became calm. They had done all they could to avoid violence. Hardy had sought the fight, and was responsible for his own death. He just had not understood that people could not be pushed beyond the limits of their endurance.

By supper a group of men had begun to negotiate with Percy. He gave in to their demands with little struggle. After Hardy's death, and in the face of the solid unity of the men, there was little else that Percy could do. On their insistence, he signed a document in the presence of everyone stating that he would recognize the union and in future negotiate with union representatives on all major issues. The shantymen had won complete victory.

The next morning a number of basic decisions had to be made to organize the work of the rest of the season. Within a matter of days the ice on the lakes would break up, the snow would melt and the roads would be impassable. Not only did Percy want to get back down the Opeongo Line but there were a number of men who did not intend working on the log drive and they also wanted to head home. It was agreed that the group leaving the shanty would go together and take Hardy's body with them. Once they got down the Opeongo Line they would all go to the police in Renfrew and give a detailed explanation of the circumstances surrounding Hardy's death. It was also agreed that those left to work on the log drive would have no foreman go with them. The men would handle everything co-operatively.

The fifteen men who were signing off the crew worked frantically that day to assemble their gear, and the next morning, an hour before dawn, they said their goodbyes. O'Riley flipped his reins over the backs of the horses and the three sleighs moved out of the camp. Strung out behind them were the horses and oxen that they were taking to be wintered at the Whitney Stopping Place.

For the twenty-five remaining shantymen there was much work left to do around the camp and less than three weeks to do it all. The first priority was to finish the log chute. Fortunately the twenty-five yards of chute left to build were no more than ten feet high and the men could hoist the heavy logs by hand, but it was still backbreaking work.

John and Meg were assigned to help Mrs. Ferguson prepare the food for the log drive. She had to calculate how much would be needed for the six-week drive and package it into tight-fitting hogsheads. What food was left over was then buried deep in the ground by one of the older shantymen who was summering at the camp.

There were a hundred other jobs that needed to be done. The men followed the log drive in boats about fifteen feet long, called pointers. As soon as the ice had melted away from the shore they had to be taken out of storage and sunk in the lake so the wood strips would swell and the boats would not leak when the drive began. The harnesses had to be cleaned and stored and the tools had to be put away for the next season. Even the canvas tents had to be carefully inspected and, when necessary, repaired. When they were finished all of these chores they still had a week or more before the ice had melted sufficiently for the drive to begin.

One lunch time, when Meg was out of the shanty, John pleaded with the men to be allowed to work on the log drive as a riverman and not just a cook's help. They agreed to let him, providing he proved he could do the work.

Meg was furious when she found out. Now her brother would get the chance to work the river while she was stuck as the cook's help. That night after supper she told everyone in no uncertain terms that she could be a riverman just as well as her brother. "It's not fair," she said. "Just because I'm a girl I get stuck to be the cook's help while John gets to be a riverman. If you let him do it then I'm going to be a riverman and no one's going to stop me!"

Not one of the shantymen dared to argue with Meg's fiery temper. There could be no doubt that she was as capable as her brother, and if one was allowed to do the work then it was only fair that the other be given an equal chance. It was quickly agreed that as long as both of them could prove themselves capable they could work as rivermen for the rest of the season.

The key to success of the log drive was to start at the highest possible point of the spring flood; then the swollen rivers would do much of the work of flushing the timber downstream. Hour by hour the men studied the river, waiting for just the right moment to start. Finally, one morning at the end of April, everyone walked to the outlet of the lake. The river seemed huge, surging so powerfully that the waterfall sent spray for a hundred yards. That day there was no debate. The shantymen agreed unanimously that the drive should begin.

It took more than an hour to cut through the rock with picks and bars to open a channel of water leading to the log chute, but when it began the water rushed down the spillway with a frightening roar. The men sent up a cheer. That chute was the fruit of a season's back-breaking work, and it was a point of pride to see the water rushing down it. But the celebration did not last long. Some of the men went out in the lake with their pointers and with the use of pikes began guiding the timbers into the chute. Each squared timber would come point-first toward the chute and then be drawn more and more into the current until suddenly it would tip upwards and enter the spillway. With a roar the log would accelerate down the whole length of the chute, bouncing from side to side until finally it splashed with an enormous shower of water into the fast-flowing waters of the Madawaska below. The timber would barely hesitate before it was caught in the current of the river and be swept downstream.

After all the timber had gone down the chute, the men eased the pointers, filled with provisions and tools, down the log run. Gangs of ten and fifteen men stood at the top of the chute and slowly lowered the boats down the spillway using long ropes. Finally, after everything had been lowered to the river, the men dammed up the water to stop it from running all season.

It was after nightfall when a group walked from the top to the bottom of the chute where Mrs. Ferguson had set up camp. In spite of their exhaustion there was not one of them who did not feel a sense of exhilaration to think that the log drive had begun.

The drive represented many things to the shanty-men: it was the start of a new round of activities, it was the end of the isolation of camp life, it meant, with each turn of the river, that they were getting closer to their homes; and for many, the log drive was the final and ultimate test of their courage and skill as shantymen. That night John and Meg felt a part of all of those things.

After a fitful sleep on the half-frozen ground, the men were up before the dawn, ate a hurried breakfast, climbed into their pointers and followed the logs down-stream. At every bend of the river some of the logs had washed ashore, and a crew would have to get out and, using their heavy poles, roll the logs back into the river again. By midday the pointers were stretched the whole ten miles from below the log chute to the point where the river emptied into Lake of Two Rivers. The cook and one of the older shantymen, who had taken the job of cook's help, were first with most of the supplies, and they hurriedly set up camp at the mouth of the river and began preparing the evening meal. A small log jam had formed in some shallow water near a group of islands, and it took an hour's work for a half a dozen men to free them, but by nightfall the river had been cleared and all of the men had made it to the camp.

A different technique had to be used to get the logs across the lake. If they waited for the current to drift the logs to the other side, it would take months to complete the drive. The shantymen broke into two teams. One hurriedly made a huge log boom large enough to enclose all of the timbers that had been cut. The other crew built a square raft out of timbers, and on it they set up the large capstan they had been carrying. They paddled the raft out into the middle of the lake and firmly anchored it in shallow water near an island. Then they took a long rope leading back from the capstan to tie securely around the boom. The capstan was a large spool-shaped cylinder that revolved when the men turned it by pushing on the long poles that projected out of the centre. The men walked around and around and slowly wound the rope around the capstan, gradually pulling the huge log boom towards the raft. The men took turns at the exhausting, monotonous work, ten at a time turning the capstan, and slowly they winched the boom up to the raft and then moved the raft ahead, anchored it, and began winching again. Finally, two days after they had started, they had winched the logs to the end of Lake of Two Rivers.

The next few days were so exhausting that Meg and John wondered if signing on for the log drive had been wise. When they got to the end of the lake they broke up the boom and drove the logs down to Whitefish Lake. Then it was back to the capstan raft for what seemed to be days and days of winching the enormous boom. Finally at the end of Galeairy Lake they released their logs into the powerful waters of the Madawaska.

It was not surprising that the log run was considered the most dangerous part of the shantyman's life. Anyone who fell into those surging waters could be dragged under by the current. The heavy woollen clothing of a shantyman would soak with water, and his big boots would make him sink like a stone. It would take good luck and superhuman strength to come out alive, and it was not surprising that there were a number of shantymen who never returned home after the annual log run.

Both John and Meg stuck to their jobs with grim determination. No one would say that they were not good workers. From sunup to sundown they were in pointers sweeping the river for timber that had gone ashore. At rapids and waterfalls log chutes had been built and log booms had been strung across the river to catch the timber. As soon as all of their logs had been trapped the chute would be opened and the shantymen would begin guiding the logs into it with their long pike poles. It was dangerous work. The men would often leave their pointers and run across the squared timbers to free a log, knowing full well that if they fell into the water they could be swept under the boom and into the waterfall before they could get a handhold.

The final test came in the fourth week of the drive. A few of the experienced men knew that they were coming to a treacherous part where the river narrowed and was pitted with small islands and rocks. John and Meg went with them ahead of the logs, and they positioned themselves on the rocks and river bank with their long pike poles to help steer the logs through the narrows. About a quarter of the logs had passed through when suddenly one lodged sideways, jamming up against two rocks across the flow of the river. Within moments other logs hurtling along behind got caught and a twisted pile of timbers grew as each log added to the numbers.

"Jam! Jam!" the men shouted up and down the bank, and as the news spread every man ran to the spot as fast as they could. The most dangerous of all possible things had happened.

John stood beside the others, holding onto his pike pole and listening to the men anxiously debating what to do. He studied the jam in every detail. The key log, that the others were all wedged into, could be seen quite clearly. If a man could get into the water, he thought, and lift one end of the timber up and over the rock, it would slip away downstream and the whole jam should tumble free. The sooner it was done, the less the risk, because there would be fewer timbers in the jam. John did not hesitate a moment. He explained to the others how he thought the jam could be freed, then bound a rope around his waist, took a heavy pole, and waded into the cold, swift-flowing water.

Meg was there and was about to protest, but even by then there was little she could do except stand with the others and slowly play out the rope that was around her brother's waist. The current was up to his thighs, surging so strongly that he had to lean against his heavy pole to hold his balance, but he waded on until finally he was by the rock and the key timber. The jam was huge, a tangled mass of logs towering over his head. He leaned into the water to make sure his heavy pole was hooked in exactly the right place, then he heaved upwards, pushing with every ounce of strength that he had in his sinewy body. Slowly, ever so slowly at first, the squared timber lifted upwards, until gradually the end came out of the water a trifle, hesitated, and then began to slip across the top of the rock that it had been wedged into.

Suddenly, John felt the timber give away. He glanced back. The jam was moving towards him, logs tumbling down on top of him as the bottom slipped out. He dropped the heavy pole and started the dash for shore. Suddenly, the rope around his waist came taunt as the men frantically dragged his body wildly through the water towards the shore. John was hit by a log, then another, but finally, miraculously, he felt himself being dragged over hard ground. He looked back; the jam had broken with a deafening roar as the logs suddenly surged downstream.

The men surrounded John, exuberantly congratulating him. Breaking a jam was the most dangerous job that a shantyman was ever called on to do, and few men had the strength or nerve to do it. Over and over again the men shook his hand and slapped him on the back, telling him what a great shantyman he had become. It was only Jacques and Cameron who disapproved. Over the season's work they had come to feel responsible for the two children of their dead friend, and although they marvelled at John's daring they scolded him that night after supper, and told him in no uncertain terms that he was not to take such risks again.

The following days were exhausting, but finally, in early June, they came to the point where the river emptied into Lac des Chats, a widening of the Ottawa. This was the end of the log drive on the upper river, and the men celebrated in traditional fashion by going into Arnprior, the logging town at the mouth of the Madawaska, and drinking and partying the night away. They had much to celebrate.

Percy's accountant had come up from Ottawa. He paid off those men who were leaving the drive and hired on a number of skilled raftsmen who were mainly French-Canadian.

Using about ten members of the original crew, they began frantically to build the rafts for the long trip down the Ottawa and St. Lawrence Rivers to the markets at Quebec City. Both Cameron and Jacques were staying on for the rafting, and although John and Meg were paid off it was agreed they could stay on with the crew until they rafted down to the Chaudière Falls in the city of Ottawa.

Rafting was the most complicated part of the log drive. On the upper reaches of the watershed the timbers were run down the rivers as loose logs, but once they reached the Ottawa the logs were built into huge rafts to be floated downstream. The most basic unit of the raft was the crib, made up of the enormous squared timbers. The raft was made up of between a hundred and one-hundred-and-fifty of these cribs, laid ten across and as many deep. When it was finally finished it was an enormous floating pile of squared timber that was still loosely enough tied together to give some flexibility, but so strong that it would rarely break apart even in the roughest waters of the St. Lawrence.

It took four weeks to build one large raft containing all of the timber that the crew had cut at the Cache Lake shanty that season. When they were finally finished, early one hot afternoon in mid-July, a small steam skow that plied the waters of Lac des Chats threw a line onto the raft and slowly towed them southeast down towards the spot where the Ottawa drained the lake. They tied up overnight, and in the morning they began to break up the rafts and run the cribs down the timber slide that skirted Chats Falls.

Running the cribs was exciting work. Three men would get onto a crib and pole it into position. The slide was twenty-six feet wide and the crib was twenty-five-and-a-half feet wide, and the men had to aim the crib skilfully so that it fitted perfectly. If, by accident, it lodged sideways at the slide intake it could take hours to free because the force of the water wedged it in tight, but the rivermen were so skilled they rarely got the cribs hung up. They made it seem so easy. As they got lined into position the water sucked them into the slide, and with a roar they rumbled down the wooden spillway, out onto the apron and then into the still waters below. On the other side of the slide another crew of men would be busy rebuilding the raft, and the rivermen would walk back over the portage to get another crib.

It took two days to take the raft through the slide at Chates Falls and reassemble it on the other side. Then they were headed downstream once again. Meg and John were not working, and they had a lot of time to sit in the warm June sunshine and watch the men skilfully steer the huge raft down the river. They were close to home now. On the east side of the river were the familiar Gatineau Hills, looking like big tree-covered humps away off in the distance, and on the west bank the gently rolling landscape was spotted with farms.

It seemed a strange experience to be so close to home after being away for so many months. The two of them lay on their backs in the hot summer sun thinking about the events of the winter. Both of them were going back home very different people from when they had left such a short time before.

It was not long before the current brought them down to Chaudière Lake, and again a small steam tug towed them towards the falls. They were in the city of Ottawa now, and as they came close to the Chaudière Falls they could see the newly completed Parliament Buildings standing high up on the hill overlooking the river, and the familiar lumber and papermills at the falls. Although they could not see it, La Breton Flats, Meg and John's home, was not a mile away. They were anxious to get off the raft, but the men started work immediately breaking up the rafts to run the log slide and there was no way of getting ashore.

Cameron saw the two of them standing on a crib waiting to get off, and immediately knew their dilemma. He waved to get their attention and shouted for them to bring their gear. John and Meg made their way forward until they were up in front with the men dismantling the raft. Suddenly Cameron was shouting to the others that Meg, John, Jacques and himself would run the first crib down the slide.

In a moment the four of them were on a free-floating crib drifting toward the slide. "Grab yourself a pole there, Meg, John!" Cameron shouted. "We're moving."

The four of them cautiously poled the crib closer and closer to the slide intake, pointing the crib into the current.

"Hold her careful, Meg!" Jacques shouted.

"You two guide her in!" ordered Cameron.

John and Meg were in front steering the crib gently by pushing on one side and then the other. It picked up speed with the current. John gave it a last touch to bring it into place, and suddenly the crib was tipping up and into the slide. With a loud rush of water, and a rumble as it skidded over the logs, the crib accelerated down the slide. The four of them whooped and shouted in the sheer joy of such a wild ride. With an enormous shower of water the crib slid out onto the apron and finally was drifting in the quiet waters below the falls.

Meg and John both felt a real sense of conflict. It was good to be back home, but they were leaving a brotherhood that had formed after months of sharing hardship and danger. It would be hard to find such friends again.

Cameron poled ashore and tied the crib by a wharf. The four of them talked quietly, knowing that they had to say goodbye but unable to express their feelings for one another. Finally they grew silent, and the time hung almost as an embarrassment. Suddenly, with a childish impulse, John hugged his two friends and ran up the portage towards the bridge. "Come on, Meg!" he shouted to his sister.

In a moment Meg did the same. Giving both the shantymen a kiss on the cheek, she picked up her gear and followed her brother. They ran all the way to the Chaudière Bridge, leaving the two far behind. There they paused, watching the two shantymen trudge over the portage back to the raft above the falls. When they came within earshot John and Meg waved. "See you next fall!" Meg shouted.

The men waved back. "We'll be there!"

John and Meg walked through the streets of La Breton Flats, the excitement of the homecoming building in both of them. They walked past children they knew playing on the street, but went unrecognized. When they turned into their own street they passed neighbours out in their yards who looked at them in puzzlement as if they felt they should know these two strong healthy looking young people but were unable to place them. Finally they came up the walk of the small neat workingman's cottage where their mother and the younger children lived. For a moment they almost opened the door and walked in as if they had never been away, but somehow they felt uncomfortable, and hesitated for a moment. John knocked on the door with his fist. There was a wait, then a fumbling on the other side, and when the door opened it was their mother, the still-strong shantyman's wife they had left so many months before.

For a long moment the three of them stood looking at each other as if in disbelief. Then John said quietly, "We've come home, mother."

Tears were coming down her face as she hugged her two oldest children. "You've come home! You've come home! Thank God you've come home safely."

EPILOGUE

IN spite of the efforts and the hopes of the shantymen in Percy's camp in the season of 1873, the union did not succeed. The following season the Percy Lumber Company went bankrupt, not because of the activities of the union, but because a depression hit the lumbering industry and Percy did not have the resourcefulness to ride it out. With the death of the company came the end of the effort to organize the Shantyman's Union.

That is not to say that all the efforts of the shantymen that season were a failure. It was one part, and an important part, in the development of a feeling by the men that they did not have to put up with the arbitrary rulings of ruthless foremen. It was another thirty years before the men in the bush were finally organized, but it would never have happened without men such as these, who created the environment for the union to finally win the allegiance of all the shantymen.

But by the time the union finally came, the squared timber trade was finished. The last raft of squared timbers was floated down the Ottawa in 1903. For a hundred years the lumber companies had plundered the forests in the Upper Ottawa Valley, and they did not stop until the best stands of timber had been completely ravaged.